From Whence Cometh Wars

Jonathan Almanzar

AmErica House
Baltimore

First printing

ISBN: 1-58851-220-7
PUBLISHED BY AMERICA HOUSE BOOK PUBLISHERS
www.publishamerica.com
Baltimore

Printed in the United States of America

This book is dedicated to my parents.
David and Robbi

Chapter 1

Jerry was dreading tonight. After five 15 hour work days, he just wanted to go home, relax and not have to entertain guests. Especially the Lesiks. *A deacon is given to hospitality,* he kept reminding himself. *But tonight?*

Holding his copy of Sporting News over his head, he left the protection of the canopy and made a leap, trying to clear the Mississippi River that now ran in front of his shop. No luck. Splash down right in the middle of the storm drain puddle. He could feel the water seeping in through his shoelaces and filling his socks. One more leap and he landed safely by his car. It was unusually rainy, especially for July, but Jerry didn't mind too much. It had been good for business. Sliding into his car, he started it up and quickly tuned his radio to the Rockies game. *Ahh*, the fifth inning had just started. At least he'd catch some of the game.

Pulling into the drive Jerry hit the garage door opener and saw Rachael's car taking up both spots in the garage. It wasn't even supposed to be parked in the garage. He slammed his car in park and sprinted to the front door splashing water chin high all along the way.

"Pameeellaa!" Jerry trumpeted in his best Fred Flintstone imitation.

"Jerry, I'm glad you're home. I have a favor to ask." He followed the voice to the kitchen where an exasperated Pam handed him a list and continued. "Could you run to the store real quick and pick these things up for me? I still have biscuits to make and a cake. Thanks honey." Pam dismissed him with a quick kiss.

"Couldn't you have sent Rachael?" He asked, not yet resigned to going.

"Oh she left with Cassie right after work for their lock-in tonight. Did you forget?"

"Yeah, I guess I did. Can I go in about 20 minutes?"

"Honey, I really need them now."

"Fine." Jerry growled.

He glanced at the list then headed to the door. He noticed the rain had finally let up. Stepping outside, and squinting from the blinding sun, Jerry saw two rainbows in the sky. They were faint but becoming more vibrant with every second that passed.

"Only in Colorado." He whispered to himself.

Turning his car onto Broadway the parade of commercials finally ended just in time for him to arrive at Jacks Grocery. He sat in his car long enough to hear the score. Rockies up 2-0 heading into the bottom of the seventh. He looked his list over one more time and formulated his plan of attack for gathering all the items as quickly as possible, starting from the back and moving crisscross toward the check out line. If his plan worked, he'd be back by the top of the 8th. Well as luck would have it, the bottom of the 9th had begun and the Rockies were down 3-2.

"Unbelievable!" Jerry shouted, surprised by his own anger.

Backing his car out and heading towards home, Todd Helton came up to the plate with one out and runners at the corners. He could feel the butterflies in his stomach as he pleaded with the radio.

"Come on Todd please, please."

The ringing of his cell phone interrupted his groveling.

"Hello." Jerry answered in a staccato tone.

"Jerry, where are you at?"

"I'm turning on to Catalpa Street right now." Jerry's mind was trying to separate Pam's words from the radio's, when he heard the familiar:

"And it ain't comin' back. A walk-off home run by Todd Helton…" He wanted to scream.

"Okay?...Jerry?" Pam's voice jerked him from Coors Field to Catalpa Street.

"That's fine honey." Jerry said trying to replay their conversation in his mind. "See you in about five minutes. I love you."

"Love you too. Bye."

"Bye."

Two blocks from home, Jerry saw the Lesik's Expedition parked in front of his house.

"Amazing." he whispered aloud.

Even after a rain, it looked like it had just come from being detailed. It always looked like that. He slid his car in behind theirs and noticed how beautiful his lawn looked. It looked like a 3D cartoon with the sun magnifying through the rain, and every blade of grass looking as if it just got out of the shower.

Tonight might not be so bad after all, Jerry thought, grabbing the groceries and heading towards the door. *Maybe we can eat out back and they'll go home at dark and*

I can watch Helton's home run on ESPN. No sooner had that thought crossed his mind than he heard Adam Lesik's booming laugh coming from inside the house. Jerry cringed, took a deep breath, and plunged in smiling from ear to ear.

"Let me give you a hand with those," Adam said as soon as Jerry stepped into the foyer. "It's good to see you, how have you been doing? Business up I bet with all this rain."

He had to admit, the Lesik's were lethal when it came to conversation. They worked together perfectly like Boris and Natasha or Bonnie and Clyde. Adam would strike first, firing question after question like a machine gun, rat-a-tat-tat, and all the while Candy just sat back, blending in with the scenery, waiting for you to begin answering Adam's barrage of questions and then like a sniper, deliver the deadly shot at just the right time. *Not tonight though.*

"Fine." He said. Short, concise, no room for interpretation, no opening for a sniper bullet.

Adam grabbed the groceries from Jerry's arms and headed towards the kitchen talking over his shoulder.

"Did you see that Rockies game? I'm not a big fan, but a home run in the bottom of the ninth. Whew!"

"Where did you see it?"

"Oh, in your living room. Pam had it on so we watched the end. Pretty exciting huh."

"Yes." Jerry said, trying to hide his jealousy.

Pam came out of the kitchen and grabbed the groceries. "Dinner will be ready in about twenty minutes, so you boys can go out back and talk if you'd like."

Adam and Jerry headed out back and exchanged small talk for a while. After a couple uncomfortable moments of silence, Jerry finally took the bait.

"So, how's the real estate business?" As soon as the word business left his mouth, he knew he wouldn't have to think up any more conversation for a while.

He could tell from the start, this wasn't the typical 100-meter sprint Adam liked so much, but a 10K cross-country conversation. Adam started out early pacing himself with the usual 'Good, good, real estate seems to be picking up around here, could be better though.' But by the six mile mark he had kicked it into high gear, explaining the growth rate, making an offer on their house, 'letting them in on' two different can't-miss opportunities, and then crossing the finish line with:

"But God's in control. He's really been blessing."

"Sounds like it," Jerry outwardly agreed. "Maybe we should go check on dinner."

"Sure. Smells delicious. Everyone knows Pam's a great cook."

"Yeah, she is."

They had a lovely dinner, with the food being outstanding as usual. Not only does Pam's food taste great, but it's always so decorative. Their conversation had been surprisingly pleasant, with Pam delivering a couple of her hilarious anecdotes. Adam and Candy were unusually gracious and even seemed to be enjoying their simple stories and interests. Maybe Jerry had misjudged the Lesik's. Maybe his impression had been a bit naïve. He had always seen them as self-involved, gossiping thirty-somethings who thought they were on Melrose Place. Tonight, however, they seemed to have some depth. They were genuinely curious about Jerry's dry cleaning business, Pam's garden, Gerry's cheerleading, and Rachael's boyfriends.

Jerry and Pam had become so absorbed in their own stories they were like two jockeys racing for position. Their focus fell on their next move, or their next story, completely oblivious to their surroundings, only listening for a key word to segue into their next tale. Reality, however, struck them at the same time. Jerry couldn't pinpoint it exactly, it could have been Adam clearing his throat, or Candy shifting in her chair, or maybe the air conditioner had kicked on, but whatever happened, it jerked them back to reality. Jerry saw Pam blush and glance at her plate, but quickly regain composure.

"Desert anyone?"

"Sure." everyone replied. Jerry tried to calculate how long it had been since someone other than him or Pam had talked. It had been long enough to be embarrassing.

They moved to the living room and Pam brought out French Silk pie and coffee.

"So, how's your real estate agency doing, Adam?" Pam was obviously trying to even out the conversation. Jerry got comfortable, bracing himself for the marathon when Adam jumped in, starting halfway to the finish line:

"Well as I was just telling your husband, Tom Dye just passed away. He owned Valley Rental. His family all lives back east and they don't want the hassle of a bunch of rentals. It would be too hard living that far away, so they are wanting to get rid of them quickly. I asked them about selling them in packages at maybe a discount rate. They agreed, so Candy and I talked it over and we made an entry level bid for the whole bunch of them. I'll admit, we grossly under bid, but they accepted."

Here Candy interrupted. "We really feel like God put this in our lives for a chance to help some people in our church. We would like to open it up for a few investors. You guys came to our mind immediately. You do so much in the church and you are both so loving and giving, you deserve an opportunity like this. We don't want you to feel pressured, but just take some time, talk it over and pray about it. Adam has all the figures in his office. If you want to stop by and pick up a copy, you are more than welcome. We are thankful God has given us a chance to help."

They finished their desserts, talked a little about the weather, the food, and a little about church. Just generalities nothing specific. A lot like the closing prayer at church, or grace before dinner. Just the motions and no real feeling beyond that. Jerry began to wonder if his whole prayer life had digressed to this. Small talk around a coffee table with someone he didn't have much in common with other than church.

They said their good byes and walked the Lesiks to the door, remaining there until the blue Expedition pulled away from the curb. Flipping off the porch light Pam went to work in the kitchen, while Jerry retired to the den. He didn't realize exactly how tired he felt until his feet were swept off the floor by his Lazy-Boy footrest. His left hand instinctively moved to the coffee table and snagged the remote, submitting it then to the authority of his right, he flipped the T.V. on just in time to hear "Na-na-naht, na-na-naht."

As soon as the Rockies highlights came on, the guilt came with it. Jerry knew he would head to bed right after this and he hadn't read the Bible today. Or yesterday. Had he read it all week? He couldn't remember for sure. He tried forcing it out by saying "it's false guilt," he tried loosening its grip by saying "as least I prayed." Finally, he broke and decided to set his alarm early, get up and have his quiet time. Even saying this, in his mind he knew he probably wouldn't get up, but at least it appeased the guilt for now.

As soon as Helton's ball landed in the rock pile, the guilt came back. This time with a different face. The face of Pam. The face of Pam cooking, the face of Pam clearing dishes, and now the face of Pam cleaning the kitchen. Was seeing the home run worth it? It never was afterwards, but the anticipation, that's where priorities get blurred. He headed to the kitchen but Pam had already finished.

"You're a jerk." he condemned himself under his breath. "Ten minutes is all it would have taken."

* * * *

The rain had ended nearly twenty minutes ago, but James didn't seem to notice. Standing now in the spot where he had spent the last forty-five minutes on his knees, he wiped the tears from his eyes looking out over the city for which he had just been to battle. Every

evening Pastor Knoll came to this spot to pray for the town of Lendel, but tonight was a little different. James had been to war. He might not
have known why exactly, and he couldn't quite explain what he felt, but he had been in the midst of spiritual warfare and emerged victorious. At least for today.

From this point on Skyline Drive, James could see the entire town of Lendel, except the steel mill. It had been built, for aesthetic purposes, behind Liberty Point. Lendel, in James mind, was the perfect small town. It covered a lot of land area for a town of just over forty thousand. The yards were large, the parks big, the two golf courses, one 18 holes the other a night-lit 9, were beautiful, and the weather, for having all four seasons, was perfect. The Rocky Mountains bordered it on every side with Denver just 80 miles to the northeast and Colorado Springs 60 to the southeast. The summers were in the mid-80's with surprisingly mild winters. They would get 6-8"of snow in December and January, but February usually picked up the slack landing 10-14."

He loved to look out across the city, to the hospital, airport, and from here, he could even see the progress they were making on the Wild West Zoo. Today however, the downtown area looked absolutely magnificent. The tall old Carthage stone buildings sparkled from the rain, reminding him of the Emerald City on the Wizard of Oz.

Something unusual caught James' eye. Two rainbows in the same sky. Each so defined, so vibrant, so distinct.

"Double promise," slid through James lips.

After staring at the rainbows until his eyes hurt, James looked down as he did every night, to the church nestled against the base of Skyline Ridge, and Mountain View Bible Institute right behind it. James said a brief prayer for every member of his staff, the deacons, and the trustees. Each individual, each personal. With a deep sigh, and one last look, James hopped in his car and headed down the windy drive. He always felt so refreshed and rejuvenated after spending this time with God, but tonight he felt drained. Physically and mentally exhausted. Weary from battle, but reassured in the promises of God.

James usually took his time on the way home, but today he needed to rush. He had to beat Hannah there and get the table set, pull the roast out of the oven, and start the brown-n-serve rolls. She had gone to pick up their youngest son from Denver. He had gone to a basketball camp and stayed with their oldest son Robert. Robert worked as the college director at a large church in Denver and he and his wife Denise, had been married for four years. They had two boys 13 months apart. James thought it would be nice if he cooked dinner for Hannah tonight rather than her having to cook after she got home.

He wasn't fast enough, however, and as he pulled into the drive, he saw Hannah through their kitchen window. He shut the car off and just watched his beautiful wife for a moment. He could see her singing as she always did, her long blonde hair falling on her shoulders, her beautiful brown eyes, and her face shining with happiness. It, no SHE, was infectious. Her singing made everyone sing, her laughter made everyone laugh, and when she cried you couldn't keep from crying. James thanked God again for giving him such a wonderful wife. He felt as though he couldn't thank God enough. Searching for words but realizing the words have never and could never be said to express his gratitude. Words would only put a limitation on his thanks and love for his wife. He finally got out of the car and decided to head in through the kitchen door rather than the front. As he opened the door, two arms greeted him wrapping around his neck.

"Oh I'm glad you're home honey. Thanks for starting dinner." Hannah said squeezing him tightly then letting go.

"I'm glad you're home too, hun. That was a quick trip."

"Yeah, it didn't take as long as I thought it would at the radio station. I just showed them my driver's license and they gave me the tickets. It was really easy. Won't Jerry be surprised?"

"Definitely. Can I see them?" James asked.

He felt like a little kid looking over the tickets to the all-star game. He still couldn't believe Hannah had won those tickets and that they were going to be in San Diego during the time of the game. *Oh well, Jerry will enjoy them more anyway.* James just wished he could see his face when he found the tickets.

"Where's Jason?" James asked placing the tickets on the counter.

"He's on the phone with Jackson."

"Or is it Cassie?" James joked.

Hannah laughed. "No it's Jackson. He really wanted him to go to the camp."

"Did he have a good time?"

"A good time? That's all I heard about on the way home. Well until we drove by the church and then his conversation changed to the lock-in tonight."

"I almost forgot about that. I want to talk to him before he leaves."

"Good, you'll probably enjoy his stories more."

James smiled and turned to head upstairs to Jason's room. He noticed the table had already been set, he looked back to see Hannah putting the rolls in the oven. He just shook his head. *Oh well, it's the thought that counts.*

He took the steps two at a time racing up the staircase and made an immediate left when he reached the summit. He heard Jason hanging up the phone and moving toward the door. James only had seconds to react. No chance to think about it, or plan it out, just pure reaction. He took two silent but gracefully large steps toward the right, then pressed his back against the wall of the bathroom. Holding his breath he tried becoming the shadows, disappear, invisible to the naked eye. He could hear Jason's steps, he could even hear the brushing sound of his pant legs as they rubbed together, two more steps…one more. James had to act now or the moment would be lost forever. Mustering all his energy, he leaped from the shadows with a horrific growl.

"Blaaaahhhh!"

Jason jumped two feet high and landed three feet closer to his room.

"Oh my gosh Dad, you scared me to death."

"Sorry Jace." The apology had little effect with James bursting at the seams with laughter. "So," James asked quickly gaining composure, "how was camp?"

"Ah man Dad, it was great."

"Did you learn anything?"

"Yeah, but the best parts were the scrimmages. I improved a lot in five days. In fact I scored 26 points in our last scrimmage."

"Serious?" James asked, surprised and proud all in one emotion.

"I just got pretty hot from the three point line and I even had a dunk. This one kid on our team was going crazy and I threw him a couple oops. Man could he fly."

"Did any coaches talk to you?"

"Supper's ready!" Hannah's voice broke up the conversation.

"We're coming!" James announced loudly.

Racing down the stairs Jason beat his father to the table.

"Are we expecting company?" Hannah asked.

"No why?"

"Well I was just wondering since you put in this whole big roast."

"No…I just…I thought it would be enough."

"For the rest of the week." Hannah started laughing, "you're so funny James."

"Thanks," quickly changing the subject he asked, "Would you like to pray, Hannah?"

Hannah nodded. "Dear Lord, thank you for our safe trip, and this food we are about to eat and will be eating until we leave for vacation. Amen."

After the snickering wasover, James asked his prior question.

"Did any coaches talk to you?"

"A couple, but the coach from Colorado Baptist watched my final scrimmage and he seemed real interested. That would be pretty cool since Robert said it's probably the best Christian school in the state…well except Mountain View."

"It is a good school. That's pretty exciting, Jace."

Jason continued with stories from camp until time to leave for the lock-in.

"Ready to go?" James asked.

"Actually I think Rachael and Cass are gonna pick me up. In fact they should be here any minute."

"What about Jackson?"

"He's still at his Uncle's in Pueblo."

"Alright then. Have fun. Your mom and I are going for a walk."

"I will. See you in the morning."

Chapter 2

"Thanks for the ride dad." Gerry said squeezing Jerry's neck one last time before grabbing her backpack and getting out of the car.

"Be careful hun. You've got your Bible right?"

"Right."

"And your inhaler?"

"Yes."

"And money? Mom gave you some money, didn't she?"

"Yes dad I'll be fine. Don't worry."

"Okay have fun." Jerry encouraged reluctantly, but Gerry didn't need much encouragement.

She rushed off towards the bus and Jerry could hear giggling as she stepped on. *Two weeks is an awfully long camp* he thought, *at least Angela's going.* Forcing himself to turn on his car and pull away from the church, Jerry decided to stop by Adam's office. It wasn't far from here and his curiosity about the investment got the better of him.

He turned onto Broadway and glanced down at his clock. 11:45. *Two more hours til the Rockies game.* This is a nice week for vacation. He'd actually get to watch a couple Rockies games. Pulling into the small parking lot of Lesik Realty, Jerry saw the pastor's new car parked in front of the door. He felt a sense of pride seeing that shiny, new, silver Bonneville. It marked the first time the pastor had decent transportation since Jerry had known him and, James confided to him, the first time he had ever bought a new car.

As Jerry opened the door to get out of his car, Pastor Knoll stepped out of Adam's realty office.

"Jerry. How ya doin'?" James asked excitedly.

"Good, and you?"

"Great, great. So how's the vacation?"

"Pretty good for the first day I guess."

Pastor Knoll always had a way of making you feel comfortable. Whether it came in the confidence with which he spoke, or that he really seemed concerned about you, or the way he captivated your attention with his animated stories and gestures. He made you feel like you were part of every story. Something made you want to open up to him, or at least lower the shield of 'everything's O.K., stand-offish, small talking conversation', that is instinctively there with almost everyone else.

"You gonna watch the Rockies game this afternoon?" James asked.

"Yeah, are you?"

"I plan on it if I can finish all my running around and get packed. They're doing pretty good, I just hope the all-star break doesn't mess them up. Well I better go. Take it easy Jerry."

"O.K. You too. Have a safe trip."

"We will."

After a handshake, Jerry entered Adam's office. He looked around the small agency. He saw a receptionist, and the two full time agents besides Adam. Adam usually hired two or three high school kids during the summer time to clean houses, mow lawns, and any other small maintenance that they could handle.

"Can I help you, sir?" The receptionist asked.

"Yes, I came to see Adam. Is he in?" Jerry hadn't seen his vehicle parked out front.

"Yes sir, he's here. What's your name?" She looked up at him again.

"Oh, sorry. It's Jerry Pattison."

The receptionist placed the call and Adam came bursting through his office door shaking Jerry's hand with both of his.

"Jerry my man, what can I do for you?"

"Well Pam and I discussed your proposal and it sounds pretty good, so I just stopped by to pick up some more info."

"Good." Adam paused and glanced at his watch, "Candy's on her way over here and then we're headed to lunch. Why don't you and Pam join us?"

"Well I don't know." Even as Jerry said this, Adam handed him the phone and began dialing. After the third ring Pam picked up. *Darn*, Jerry thought, he really hoped Pam wouldn't answer. He didn't want to have to persuade her into going right in front of Adam. However, to his relief and amazement Pam said yes. He asked Adam where they were going and told Pam he would swing by and pick her up.

Jerry turned onto Catalpa Street and for the first time in the eleven years they had lived in this house, he realized why it's called Catalpa. He counted thirty-one Catalpa trees along the sidewalks on the three block stretch from the corner to his house. He had never really noticed the Catalpa's before, except in the fall when he had to pick up their pods. He hadn't really had the time to notice such things ever since buying the dry cleaning business. This would be his first vacation in three years, and his days off had been spent at church or taking his daughters to practices, work, activities, etc. He just wanted to relax, do a little yard work, watch some baseball, and play a little golf. This lunch with the Lesiks had cut into his non-scheduled day and he hoped it wasn't becoming a trend. Two meals in four days with the same couple is a lot, but with the Lesiks, it's overwhelming. They did get along pretty good the other night, however, and Pam didn't seem to hesitate at all, so maybe he's just making to big a deal out of nothing.

Jerry pulled into his drive and before he could put his car into park Pam came out of the house and jumped in.

"Wow, you seem excited." Jerry remarked.

"I am. You know I've wanted to go to Rosalina's ever since it opened," Pam said, as she pulled down the visor and began primping her hair in the mirror, "and this is my first chance."

"See, aren't you glad we waited?" Jerry smirked.

"Humph."

Pam couldn't stop talking, going on about how she heard

Rosalina's had the best vermicelli in town, how they bake fresh tortillas to order, how they roast their own green chilies, how they use real pork and not pork by-products. Jerry smiled and laughed. Pam was amazing when she gets fired up about something, rattling off all kinds of facts, hear say, and expectations. It made Jerry laugh.

"You should be on a commercial."

"Really? Oh there it is, don't miss the turn."

Jerry turned into the crowded parking lot searching for a space.

"There's one up there." Pam pointed and Jerry saw Adam and Candy standing in an empty space. Adam began motioning Jerry to pull in, pointing with his right hand, downward toward the empty space, and swinging with his left in a full circle, overhand pitching motion. Jerry pulled in and he and Pam stepped out.

"The parking lot's pretty crowded so we decided to save a place for you."

"Thanks," Jerry said gratefully, "but did anyone get mad?"

"Nah, I think everyone thought we worked here."

All four exchanged their 'how are you's and fine's' and waited for their names to be called. The wait time was quoted at twenty minutes but was closer to five.

"Wow," Pam said as she followed the hostess to their table. The restaurant covered 25,000 square feet. It looked like a giant cavern, with a dozen or so mini dining areas off in their own little alcoves. It had a waterfall, a little stream with fish and lilies, and the lighting came from the torches and lanterns all around. They were led to a table in the back of a room called Serendipity. Every table sat alone, apart from the others and Adam mentioned he used this room for business lunches.

"Very private. You can get a lot done without clients worrying about eaves droppers."

"I bet," Jerry agreed. "So what's good?"

Adam went on reciting about half the menu... "but that's all I've tried so far. I think I'll have a Smothered Machaca Azteca today."

"Sounds good to me too. How about you hun?"

"I think I'm just going to have a side of vermicelli, some tortillas and some green chili." Pam answered. Candy needed a few minutes.

After the waiter brought out the chips and salsa, Adam handed

Jerry a proposal sheet. It covered everything, from the entire list of properties, their bid, how much capital was needed from investors, an estimated P&L statement, to a return to investment ratio. The return was almost unbelievable. Pam and Jerry had discussed it the last two nights and had made a decision to invest if the return came out to be even half as good as this looked.

"How many people do you have right now?" Jerry asked. He didn't realize he had cut Adam off in mid sentence. He didn't notice, until then, that Adam had been giving running commentary the entire time.

"Well like I said, right now we have three and we need four to make it work. My parents, Candy's parents, and us. I'm meeting with a guy this afternoon about it, that's why I'm glad you guys came by. What do you think?"

"Sounds great! We would like to do this. Do you have many other people looking?"

"We've shown it to two other families, but I think one is going to say no. We'd really rather you guys buy in on this than the other couple. They're real nice but they don't go to church and well, you know."

"Keep it all in the family." Jerry joked.

"That's what the Pastor said." Exclaimed Adam.

"The Pastor?" came the simultaneous question from Jerry and Pam.

"Yeah he came in to look at some investment opportunities and I showed him this. He didn't seem too interested in it."

"Oh is that why he was there today?"

"Today? Oh, no that was something totally different. I guess Hannah and him went to look at a house out in the country somewhere. He just stopped by to give me a bid to make for him."

"A bid? Have they even sold their house yet? Is it even on the market?"

"No, and I don't think they plan to sell it. I really don't know what they are going to do with it."

"Wow that's really weird." Jerry said. Pam just sat back too stunned to say anything.

"Yeah," Adam continued, "they bought that new car, they're looking for a new house, investment opportunities, and Hannah quit her job. Maybe they inherited some money, or maybe they won the Lottery--"

"--or maybe he's stealing." Candy said. Cool and calculated. Jerry never saw the weeds move or the glint of sunlight on the barrel. He never heard the gunshot, but did feel the sniper bullet rip through his flesh and grab hold of his heart squeezing the life from him. *Stealing? Not my pastor*, thought Jerry.

"Wh-Wh-What," he stammered out.

"Oh I don't know," Candy said, crawling to a better location to get a more clean shot. "We've heard some things from a lot of different people and I'm just a little worried."

"Like who? Like what?" Jerry had recovered from the first shot just enough to be angry.

"Well, like, do you know why he left San Diego?"

"Yes, because we called him."

"Yes, but do you know why he was even interested in candidating?" Candy's speech became colder, more driven, focused in on her target. She would let him defend himself into the open, firing light rounds until his defense had worn down and then leave one that sticks.

"Yes," Jerry said.

"Why?" Candy fired back.

"I can't remember." Jerry's mind raced.

He could not remember. He could remember discussing it, he could remember hearing it, he just couldn't remember it. 'It' was blank.

"Well, I heard he was stealing from the church."

"No he wasn't." Jerry defended.

"Jerry, listen for just a second," Adam's voice sounded distraught, like it pained him to say this. "Our offerings have been down considerably over the last six Sundays--"

"–It's summertime Adam." Jerry interrupted.

"There hasn't been a deacons or trustees meeting in how long? At least six weeks. They bought a new car, they're looking for a new house, investment opportunities, they're going on vacation for ten days, and I also heard that some money is missing from the Missions Account."

"James can't even sign a church check though," came Jerry's last desperate attempt to save his pastor. He had been too focused on the rat-a-tat-tat of Adam to see Candy creep in. The setup, the kill.

"But Steve can." Candy said.

Steve had moved to Lendel eight years ago from San Diego. He and James were friends from way back and he had been the treasurer at San Diego Temple when James had been the Associate Pastor there. He got elected as treasurer of Lendel Community Church about one year ago. He is now a professor at Mountain View Bible Institute.

Jerry had no answer. This bullet had struck its mark. He could feel his heart bleeding into his stomach; the feeling made him sick. He wanted to vomit. His pastor, his friend, stealing.

By the time Jerry and Pam reached their house, Pam had already convinced Jerry that the Lesiks liked to gossip, that Pastor Knoll was not stealing, and that Jerry should call him immediately and let him know that this might be going around. Jerry was feeling pretty bad as he picked up the phone to dial Pastor Knoll's house, when he heard the familiar broken dial tone that indicated they had messages. He went ahead and called Pastor James house. After the fourth ring their machine picked up. Jerry waited and left a brief message:

"James this is Jerry. Can you give me a call whenever you get in. It's pretty important."

Jerry hung up the phone then picked it up to listen to the messages. As he listened to the message, all his doubts that had gone away were slowly creeping back in.

"Jerry, this is James. We decided to go ahead and stay at a hotel in Denver tonight and catch our plane in the morning. If you need anything, call Hannah's parents. Their number is on our table. Thanks again for feeding Oscar. There's some instructions on the table as well. Have a fun vacation."

Anybody else and this would seem like no big deal. But James, James used to make them sleep in the car on long trips or push it the whole twenty-four hours just switching off drivers. He never stayed in a hotel. It was a miracle they were even flying out to San Diego.

Jerry tried shaking the doubts out of his head, then reasoning them out, 'that's what I would do. I'd go up and stay in a hotel the night before.' But the doubts wouldn't leave. It was a standoff. He would move, they would move. He couldn't shake them neither would he yield to them. He tried placing other things, answers, in the forefront, but they constantly remained. Soaking into the background until they were the background. As long as he kept his mind occupied he was safe, but a moment's lapse, and they seized their opportunity, racing toward the front lines screaming their fears until he could head them off with mowing the lawn or a game of cards. It was a matter of time. He would either become callous to their accusations or yield to their assumptions.

* * * *

Hannah couldn't help but giggle at her husband's impression of a pack mule. He had piled all their luggage they had onto his body. He had bags around his neck, on his arms, under his arms, and on his now hunched back. Jason had offered to help, but James shrugged him off.

"No, no I'm fine. Hold the door…please, hold the door." He was stumbling like a drunkard finally crashing against the wall of the elevator. "Whew, almost there." James' words were hard to understand, but that should be expected with Hannah's handbag strap clinched tightly in his teeth.

The elevator finally stopped and the doors slid open. James came toppling out like he had been tossed from a moving car.

"Which way?" He asked. Hannah and Jason were laughing so hard by now they could hardly speak. "Which way?…Hurry!" James was now pleading.

"418." Hannah said between laughs pointing toward their room.

James turned and attempted his stumble-run-hunchback shuffle down the hall. He looked like Quasimodo the luggage salesman working his way down the hall until he found his next victim. His breaths were coming quicker and shorter, and his pace was increasing until he finally reached the threshold of 418. With a huge sigh of relief, the luggage began shedding from his body like water from a roof.

"I (gasp, huh, huh) told you we didn't (huh, huh, gasp) need a bell hop." James stammered triumphantly.

"Was it worth it dad?" Jason asked.

"Yeah. I saved $10 plus got a little exercise. My jaw is really tired feeling now though."

"Good. Maybe we will finally get to talk." Hannah's joke hit the right nerve at the right time and sent the three of them into another round of laughter. Finally gaining control, they moved their bags into the room and got settled in.

"What time are we supposed to meet Robert and Denise?"

"Not until 8 o'clock. Robert said Denise's parents were going to get in to their house at about seven, and then they were going to head straight from there to the restaurant." James answered.

"Good. I'm not real hungry yet and I think Jace wants to swim."

Denise's parents were coming in from Kansas City today to spend the rest of the week with them, and then her, Robert and the boys were heading to San Diego for the anniversary party. James still couldn't believe Hannah's parents had been married for fifty years.

"I bet they'll be surprised to see R.J. and little Jim." James didn't realize he was thinking out loud.

"Who dear?"

"Oh I was just thinking about your parents. I'm a little nervous about going back to San Diego. I didn't think I would be. I mean, it's been fifteen years, but I'm still a little nervous."

Hannah could see the concern in her husband's eyes. She could hear the distress in his voice. It had been years since she had seen him like this, and she hated to put him through it again.

"I'm sorry, honey." Hannah said remorsefully.

"Don't worry about it. I can't stay away forever. Anyway, the last fifteen years in Lendel have been worth it. Don't you agree? I mean, it's so obvious God wants us here. There's no doubt in my mind whatsoever. The Institute, the way God has blessed the church, the way both of our kids have flourished, and even Jace is thinking of a Christian college. God wants us in Lendel."

"You don't have to talk me into it Honey, I completely agree. I just wish you didn't have to go through this again."

"Thanks Hannah, but I don't really want to focus on this anymore. Sure, I'm a little nervous, but this is something really special your parents have done, and I don't want anything to detract from their moment. If a problem arises, I'll deal with it then. I just need you to know I'm a little nervous, in case I start talking to much then you'll know why and stop me."

"I love you Honey." Hannah said, her eyes filled with tears.

"I love you too." James slid over to the couch sitting down beside his wife and holding onto her. His hug, this time, was just as much of a comfort to him, as it was to her.

Chapter 3

Jerry was jerked from sleep by the phone ringing. He fumbled around trying to shut off his alarm clock before realizing it was the phone. Picking up the receiver, Jerry mumbled "Hello."

"Hi Jerry, this is Ben. Sorry, did I wake you?"

"No, No I've been up." Jerry lied. He was looking around to see what time it was. 9:50. It had been a long time since Jerry had slept in that late. Of course, it had been a long time since he had stayed up as late as he had last night. He couldn't remember what time he had fallen asleep, but the last time he looked at the clock it had read 3:38. He laid awake after that for what seemed like two hours, but might have only been 20 minutes. He didn't know for sure.

"Jerry I'm a little worried." Came the voice on the other end. "I've been getting flooded with calls the last couple of days asking about the church's mission's account, building fund and the low offerings over the past couple months. I didn't know what I should tell them so I told them to call either you or the Peter's."

"Why not the Pastor?" Jerry questioned.

"Well, it might have been a little awkward, since Pastor is the one they were sorta questioning."

"What do you mean?"

"Well several people mentioned they were concerned he might be getting a little funny with the finances."

"You mean stealing."

"Oh I don't think Pastor Knoll would steal Jerry, its just weird how so many people have been calling. And there is some money missing from the mission's account. I looked this morning."

"Have you talked to Steve?"

"I can't get a hold of him."

"Do you mind if I come down there and talk to you?"

"No problem. My day is open after 2:00. How about 2:30?"

"All right. I guess I'll see you then. Bye."

"Bye."

Jerry jumped in the shower and started getting a late start on the day. He didn't hear the phone ringing again until he shut off the water. Springing out of the shower, he slid a little on the wet floor. Regaining his balance, he snared a towel as he dashed towards the phone in his bedroom.

"Hello." He said out of breath.

"Hi Jerry its Bill...Peters."

"Hi Bill."

Bill Peters was a deacon in the church. He had grown up in Lendel but then left for college. He got involved with some big, east coast church and was even a Junior Deacon before moving back here with his wife Barbara and three kids. He had taken a job as a buyer with Lendel Steel and Fabrication. Over the last eight years, he had been instrumental both financially and spiritually to the growth of Lendel Community Church. When the time came for new appointee's for the position of deacon, Bill was a no-brainer. He was a good, young leader, and very influential in the soccer mom age group. His dad Hank, had been a member for over forty years and now served as a trustee.

"What's up?" Jerry asked.

"I just heard some pretty disturbing news."

Great, thought Jerry, *this is getting out of hand.*

"Jack Johnson just left my office and he said he had been up until 11:00 last night answering phone calls from people who are concerned that our Pastor is…well, stealing. I know it's hard to believe and you know Jack is opposed to Pastor Knoll, but he said he was fired from his church in San Diego for stealing. He also said a lot of people were wondering how they could afford a new car--"

"--wait a minute. We took up a love offering and made the down payment on that car for Pastor Appreciation Week." Jerry objected.

"He already paid it off. He just took in one lump sum and paid for the whole thing." Jerry was speechless. "Anyway, Jack thought it would be a good idea if we had a deacons meeting as soon as possible."

"We can't have a meeting without the Pastor." Jerry argued.

"It's about the Pastor, Jerry. We need to get together and at least prepare some kind of statement, for when people call us. In a way, we are helping Pastor James until we know for sure. The people will listen to you Jerry, everybody looks up to you. I really think we, as the deacons, need to sit down and discuss this."

"Alright." Jerry relented. "When would be a good time for you?"

"Tonight." Bill said firmly.

"Tonight?"

"Yes, tonight. We need to be in agreement before church tomorrow night and have some answers. I know there are going to be a lot of questions and we need to be unified."

"Alright then, tonight. I'll call Phillip and you tell Jack. What about Mark and Brad?"

"No, I don't think we should concern them until we have some idea if there's any validity to the questions."

"Yeah, you're right. See you about 7:00 then?"

"7:00 it is. Bye."

"Bye."

Jerry hung up the phone completely depressed. His doubts rushed in on him and overtook him without any fight. His hope had pulled down its flag and retreated from its city. The flag of 'doubt and sorrow' now waved in its place.

"I hope I'm wrong." Jerry said aloud, sure he wasn't.

Jerry finished getting ready, grabbed a snack bar, and backed his car out, heading to Pastor Knolls. He was glad Pam and Rachael had gone to the factory outlets today. They probably wouldn't be back until 10:00 and by then he should have some things figured out.

Jerry felt sickly nervous as he pulled into the Pastor's driveway. He could hear his stomach gurgle and a chill ran across his back. He kept telling himself: 'I'm only feeding Oscar. I'm only feeding Oscar,' but he was worried he would do more than that. He stepped up on the porch and picked up the hide-a-key rock out of the flowerpot. He fumbled with the lock until the door finally came open. He walked purposefully to the dining room not letting his eyes wander one bit. He spied an envelope with his name on it on the corner of the table. He opened the envelope and read the letter:

"Thanks again Jerry. Oscar gets a cup and a half of his food once a day. It's in the shed out back. The key is in the roll top desk. Don't worry about the plants they are all fake. Oh, the present on the table is for you.

Thanks again,

The Knolls

Jerry looked up and saw the square wrapped package. He picked it up and it felt as light as a box of Styrofoam peanuts. He decided to go ahead and open it now. Taking out his key, he split the ribbon, then carefully peeling back the corners he slid the box out. He always saved wrapping paper like that as if he might someday reuse it. To this day he never had, but he had two boxes in his attic filled with smoothed down present shells just waiting for a box their exact size.

He pulled open the flaps of the box to expose Styrofoam peanuts. *Great*. He moved over to the trash can and slowly started scraping the peanuts into it. He felt his finger nip something that felt like a picture. He secured his thumb and index finger on it and pulled it from its carton. The instant he saw what it was he couldn't believe it. Tickets to the all-star game. He dumped the rest of the box out and grabbed the two on-field VIP passes that fell into the trash can. He looked the tickets over and saw they were luxury box seats.

"Unreal." He whispered.

Jerry was completely stunned. He had no idea how James could have gotten these. *Good old James*. As soon as that thought came to his mind, it was gunned down by his doubts. It was almost like guerilla warfare in his mind now. Never knowing where the doubts would come from. No pattern, they didn't play by any rules, they just constantly attacked. Positive thoughts about the Pastor had no chance. *How could he afford the tickets and the VIP passes. It must have been at least two grand, and to just give them away*. Jerry suddenly wanted to leave. He felt compelled to leave. He slid the tickets into his shirt pocket and very quickly moved to the roll top desk. He opened it and saw the key in a cubbyhole on the right hand side. He grabbed the key and started to slide the top down when he noticed a deposit slip lying face up on the desk. At first glance, it looked like it read $130,000.00. He nearly choked, but then he picked it up. $13,000.00. Better, but where in the world would James get $13,000.00. For the first time Jerry's doubts were no more. Their tour was over, they had done their job, and their replacements had arrived and were beginning to dig deep trenches. Their flag now waved 'Reality'. Tears were rolling down Jerry's cheeks. Tears for his friend, tears for the church, and most of all, tears for himself. He knew he was the leader now and this was going to be a rough road.

* * * *

"One down twelve more to go." Brad said as he kissed Jenny goodnight, in front of her lodge. "Make sure you get plenty of sleep, and don't let Gerry and Angela keep you up all night."

"That's almost impossible. I think they giggle in their sleep."

Brad laughed and rubbed her belly one more time. "Sweet dreams."

As Brad turned to head back towards his dorm, something caught his eye. He looked out across the lighted grounds trying to see if someone was out there. It was past curfew so anyone caught was going to have to face some serious consequences. If it was who he thought, he could hear kitchen patrol calling their name.

"Shhhh." Brad held his finger up to his lips.

Jenny tried to stand perfectly still. Brad crouched down and shrunk back into the shadows. He was scanning the open area of the camp, looking for any place to hide. He tried to relocate for a better view of the area behind the chapel. Jenny bit her hand trying to hold back the laughter seeing her husband belly crawl across the pine-needle carpet floor. Brad finally got himself positioned correctly and saw two figures dart from behind the chapel and into the wooded area just behind the mess hall. They ran crouched over and moved quickly. Brad wondered if they saw him but he didn't know how they could have. He pushed himself up from the ground and returned to Jenny's side.

"You might as well go to bed. I'm gonna have to go get a

flashlight, and maybe one of the other sponsors help to go find them. It looks like we have deserters."

"You're so funny." Jenny giggled.

Brad was just like a little kid sometimes. At times, his imagination ran wild, and other times he was the most mature, levelheaded man she knew. He would make a great father, of that, she was sure.

Brad smiled "Goodnight honey."

"Goodnight."

Jenny went inside and Brad headed towards his dorm. He could hear who ever it was whispering just outside the campgrounds, but he couldn't tell exactly where it was coming from. Brad could feel the adrenaline rising. Whoever it was, acted pretty confident, almost brash with the way they were not worried about making too much noise, daring Brad to come after them. He was going to accept their challenge, and smile the whole time they washed dishes tomorrow.

He rounded up two other counselors, Kramer Binx, a trustee and the Junior High Sunday school teacher at their church, and Todd Walls, the youth pastor from Denver Christian. They hunted for an hour and a half. They got close a couple of times, close enough to almost make out the whispering. It had been constant, nearly understandable but not quite. A few times, Brad thought he heard words but couldn't make sense of it. Finally, the three men returned to their dorm, tired and frustrated.

"Let's count the kids we have in here, it should be 40, and if they're all here we know they're from someone else's dorm."

"Sounds good." Brad and Kramer agreed.

Sure enough all 40 were accounted for, so they decided to let the other counselors know about it at their leaders meeting in the morning. They needed to have them keep a better eye on their kids and maybe have a count time for liability purposes.

Brad laid his head on the pillow and before he closed his eyes, he said a brief but sincere prayer for the two kids, whoever they were.

Chapter 4

7:00 a.m. in the Rockies brought with it 40 degree temperatures, even in July. Brad had just finished his Bible study and devotion with his small group of Zealously devoted, Early morning, Bible warriors, or ZEB's for short. If they were tired at 5:30 when they left camp, the cold had made them all more awake, and a bit frisky. They had hiked about a fourth of a mile to where Turkey Creek made a sharp turn and a natural beach had formed. Facing east from this spot on the beach, you could see the most beautiful sunrise. It came over the mountain tops slowly, filling the gray sky with blistering oranges and reds. They moved in gracefully, not blinding or surprising, but gradual, like someone was painting over a drab room until the walls seemed to come alive with joy. There was nothing that could compare to the beauty of a Rocky Mountain sunrise. Not the sunset on an ocean beach, not the Northern Lights on a clear night, not the Grand Canyon, not even a rainbow after a brief shower broke up a hot summer day, nothing compared. This was God's masterpiece. There was no debating creation. One time is all it would take, and you would forever believe in Divine Creation.

Brad was awestruck. The kids were silent, as the sun was creeping up over the tops of the mountains, for a moment. The silence was broken when a lone voice broke out with "Oh Lord my God, when I in awesome wonder…" one by one voices joined until all twelve were singing 'How Great Thou Art'. One by one, the voices cracked and ended in tears until the lone voice finished the song. Brad didn't know who it was, but it didn't matter. It had been spontaneous and beautiful. The rest of the time was spent in Psalms and then praying. In that one hour on the mountain top, his small group of devoted Jr. Highers lives had been forever changed. For most of them, this was the last activity as Jr. High kids, but the memory of this camp, this morning, this sunrise service, would stay with them their entire life.

Heading down the mountain now, the cool morning air, coupled with the mind of a 13 year old, Jared Tucker decided to beat the group to camp. He hung out in the back of their group, and started falling behind. Finally, he saw his chance and cut out into the woods alone. The rest of the group continued on unaware of the disappearance of their adventuresome friend.

* * * *

Seven o'clock was approaching quickly. Jerry had been watching their grandfather clock for over an hour now. The minute hand seemed to be moving as fast as a second hand, bringing with it a sense of trepidation for what was inevitable. After tonight, the members of Lendel Community Church's lives would be forever changed. Maybe, just maybe, for the better. Jerry thought back to what Ben had said:

"I have supported the pastor from day one. I stood by his side when he decided to build the building. I stood by his side when he decided to start the institute. I stood by his side when he hired Brad, and I stood by his side when he refused to give the opening prayer at graduation last year. I stood by his side for every decision he made, never questioning his motives. Now, I have to wonder what his motive was behind everything he did. If they were impure and not from God then we have a hard road ahead of us, but the church will be better in the long run. If God could bless this church because of the hearts of our people and our leadership groups, with a, and I hesitate to say, false prophet as our leader, think what he could do when we were free from the influence of James. You have a great opportunity Jerry, to make a huge difference in the lives of so many people. But make sure you approach the situation prayerfully; if we are wrong, may God have mercy on our souls."

He had gone home immediately and prayed. He prayed until he

could pray no longer and he felt more distressed than earlier. Before, his worry was over what would happen to the church. Now, it was over, did he do it? Jerry kept reminding himself of the facts. Not only of stealing, but of maybe being a false prophet. The Bible said Satan himself could appear as an angel of light. He didn't think James was Satan, but he could bridge the gap in his own mind to a satanically misled, confused false teacher.

Jerry was now scaring himself. On one hand, he didn't want the clock to ever reach seven. He didn't want to deal with anything. Maybe if seven o'clock never came they wouldn't have to deal with it. On the other hand he wanted it to be seven now. He wanted to be around friends, praying and comforting one another. He decided to go ahead and leave. It was only 6:15 but he needed to leave, clear his mind and sort through what he wanted to say, and what he wanted to hold back until he could decide on how relevant it really was. He always thought better when he was driving, and this house was giving him the creeps anyway.

Jerry hadn't been driving but ten minutes when he noticed he was near the institute. He hadn't really been paying attention to where he was going, he had just been driving. He decided to drive through the campus then go ahead and swing by the church. Maybe he could set up some chairs and start some coffee, he told himself, all the while just hoping the pastor's office was open. He probably wouldn't look through his files, or his computer, but maybe James had left something laying around. He felt like he was preparing for a recon mission. His mind was working out the details to explain what he was doing if he got caught. It also was creating what he thought he might find. Maybe deposit slips, some kind of illegal documents, a journal, a love note from some lady in the church…where had that last thought come from? That was something Jerry never thought was a possibility before, but now, it almost seemed like he wanted to find something like that. His palms were sweaty and his heart was pounding as he turned into the church parking lot. He didn't have to worry though, he saw several cars parked in the lot including Bill and Henry Peter's trucks, and Jack Johnson's Cadillac. *They're here awfully early*, he thought.

Jerry sneaked in the back door of the church, slipping down the hall towards the offices. They were meeting in the basement so he figured he might have enough time to look through James' office before anyone came upstairs. Heading down the long corridor, he noticed a light on in the prayer room. *That's weird*, he thought. Coming closer, he looked in to see Bill Peters, Henry, and Jack sitting around a table with Adam Lesik sitting at the head.

"Jerry, come on in and join us." Adam said. " We were just getting ready to have a prayer meeting before your meeting tonight. Our church needs it."

Jerry was shocked. First of all, he didn't think anyone had seen him glance in, and secondly what was Adam doing here? Nobody was supposed to know about their meeting tonight.

"Sure." He said entering the room and taking a seat next to Henry.

What's Henry doing here? He isn't a deacon and this is supposed to be a Deacon only meeting. Even Brad and Mark, weren't told of this meeting and they're on staff. Adam interrupted Jerry's thoughts.

"We all know why we are here tonight. I think we should start the night off with prayer. Before that, however I have a few things I would like to say. I have known Pastor James for several years now. I have to admit there have been things he has done that I didn't always agree with," here he paused, "but I never said anything about them. Well to anyone else anyway. I have talked to him about things he did that I didn't think a Pastor should do but I don't think he ever really listened. I think he just heard what I had to say and that was it. However, with something like this we have to be firm. He has to listen. I know he's hard to deal with him sometimes, because of his ego and all, but we have too. This is our church. We built it, not one man; and we can't let one man destroy it."

Jerry was taken aback. Was Adam talking about the same Pastor Knoll that Jerry knew? James may have been a thief but nobody thought he was hard to talk to.

"I'll go ahead and lead in prayer," Adam continued, "we'll go around the room and then Jerry you can close."

"Alright." Jerry said bowing his head.

Adam started out thanking God for allowing them this time to get together and pray, but after that, it was all blank for Jerry. He was too busy planning his prayer, making sure he used the right words, trying to make it seem like he was humbly coming before God, yet still trying to convey his message to the men here in this room. Before he knew it, Henry was saying Amen. That was Jerry's queue. He knew everyone had already prayed so they would all be listening to his prayer. He hoped he didn't repeat anyone else, but he needed to make sure his prayer was long enough that everyone would know he was spiritual. He was searching for the emotional hook, listening for an 'Amen' or a 'Yes Lord' or even a grunt. He finally found what he was looking for. He played this chord of emotion to its brink and then closed with his usual "in Jesus name… Amen." This was followed by Amen's around the room.

"I guess we should head down stairs for our meeting." Bill said. "I'll call you tonight Adam, and let you know how it went."

"I'd appreciate it. Candy and I will be praying for you guys."

"Thanks." came from all three of the deacons.

Jerry, Bill and Jack headed downstairs to join Phillip who was already there. They all shook hands and took their seats around the table. It was a little more awkward then Jerry thought it would be with the pastor not being there, everyone just kind of sat around waiting for someone to start. Finally, Jack spoke up.

"I would like ta make a motion ta call this meetin' ta order."

"It isn't going to be a meeting like that," Bill said. "It's more of an informational meeting. We have, or may have a serious problem and we need to figure out where we stand, and what will be our M.O. in handling questions. Jerry why don't you get us started with what you know so far."

Jerry was still not positive about what he knew for sure. He was hoping he would find some answers here.

"I guess I just know what I've heard." He began rubbing the back of his neck as he continued. "There is money missing out of the missions account, James is looking to buy a new house, they paid off their car, our offerings seem to be lower than what our attendance would suggest, and I found a $13,000.00 deposit slip at his house."

"You found a what?" was the unanimous question.

"A deposit slip." Jerry hadn't realized he had even said that.

He hadn't planned on it, it just sort of slipped out unawares. He kind of regretted it, but at the same time felt relieved. It was now someone else's decision and not his alone.

"I knew it," Jack said smugly. "I knew it was jist a matter of time 'til he screwed up. I told you guys when we first thought about hirin' him he was gonna be trouble. Now we've got a mess on our hands."

"Hold on a minute." Phillip spoke up for the first time. "Has anyone talked to the pastor or are we all just jumping to conclusions? This is so out of character for him, I just think there has to be some sort of an explanation."

"Is it out of character?" Jack asked sarcastically.

Jack Johnson looked like a rookie card player holding a Royal Flush. You could see the enjoyment in his eyes. Jack was the oldest of the deacons, and yes, he had said that Pastor James would cause trouble. For fifteen years, he was wrong, but that hadn't stopped him from trying to find fault. He had become James' self-proclaimed auditor. He proudly told people his job on the deacon board was to oppose Pastor Knoll, make him work a little, sweat a little, and not get too big for his britches.

"How well do we know James? You weren't here when we hired him, Phillip. It was a split decision. He had problems in his past and some people didn't want to take a chance on him."

"I may not have been here when PASTOR James was hired, but I have watched him for the last ten years. This is out of character for him. I would have found it more believable if this meeting had been a disciplinary meeting against you for cheating on your wife than…"

"Why you…"

"Enough. This is getting out of hand. We are supposed to be the leaders, we are supposed to support one another in crisis situations, and we have to remain level headed. We have to put aside our personal feelings in this matter, for the good of the church. No one has said he has been stealing for sure, but Phillip you need to look at the evidence, not just the title on his desk." Bill's voice sounded confident and for the first time in two days Jerry felt his stomach muscles relax and his hand leave the back of his neck. He realized what a leader Bill was and that he would probably get them through this. "All of us have to put aside our prejudice one way or another. You have to forget he is the Pastor and think of him as just another man. Forget the weddings, funerals, him baptizing your children, counseling, those are just emotional attachments. We have to detach ourselves emotionally and look at this purely intellectually. It is the only fair way. It has to be us. We have to remain strong and level-headed, for the church."

"I don't know that I can do that." Phillip objected. "How can I just sever my devotion to a man that I have listened to for ten years. I have seen him baptize kids, your kids Bill. I have seen him spend the night in the waiting room of the hospital more than once with a worried family, not a single birthday or anniversary has gone by without a card or a note from him, and I have learned more from watching his life than I could from a thousand sermons by any preacher you choose. No, I don't think I can 'detatch' myself."

Jerry was staring at Phillip's face. He saw his lips move and he heard the different inflections of his voice, but the words weren't registering. He could have been speaking Chinese for all Jerry knew, he was too focused on Phillip's face. Jerry had known Phillip for thirteen years and until this day he had never realized how much Phillip looked like a weasel. The scary thing for Jerry was, the more Phillip talked the more weasel like he appeared to Jerry until he had become a weasel. Jerry's focus on Phillip's face was broken by the moment of silence between Phillip's ending and Bill's rebuttal.

The realization for Jerry was that Phillip was no longer part of their group. He had seen what he truly was, and would have to keep watch on Phillip.

The rest of the meeting continued without many objections from any of the men. Jack did get a couple more digs in on the pastor, and Bill established himself even more as a leader, but Jerry remained silent. He just watched Phillip until the group said their good byes and turned their cars homeward. He couldn't shake the feeling that Phillip was bad for their group. He wondered if he was the only one that saw it. If so, he would have to be very cautious around Phillip. The flag of realization was being lowered from the pole of Jerry's mind and 'Paranoia' was being raised double-time.

* * * *

"Jared! Jared!...Jared!" Brad voice was growing hoarse.

No one knew how long he had been gone or which way he went. Brad remembered him being there this morning at their Bible study but hadn't really looked for him the rest of the day. It was going to get dark within the hour and as soon as the sun went down, the cold air would be coming in. Jenny had helped Brad look around camp for Jared, but was now staying with the thirty-five Jr. Higher's they had brought up here. Kramer had set out from behind the mess hall where they heard the kids last night. He headed north towards Blue Lake and then swung back around west and was coming up through Falling Rock cliffs where so many kids liked to slip off too. Brad had hiked up to where they met this morning, then walked along the river a little way, finally heading back to camp. He and Kramer had confiscated a couple of walkie-talkies and were communicating back and forth. Brad was really starting to get nervous.

"Kramer. Any sign of him?"

No answer.

"Kramer...Kramer."

"Yeah Br... no...of him."

"Kramer you're breaking up. Just head back to camp"

"10-....."

Brad beat Kramer back to camp and went immediately to the lodge. Chapel had just ended and the kids would all be divided into their church groups to have a time of devotion. Their group always met in the game room at the lodge. Brad went in the door and took an immediate left down the stairs. He could hear Angela praying as he got closer. She was praying for Jared. Brad waited for her to finish and then he went on in.

"Have you found him yet?" Jenny asked expectantly.

"No. We are going to get flashlights and a couple more counselors and head out again. It's already getting kinda cool out. Keep praying."

No sooner had Brad left the lodge than he ran into Kramer. He had already found a couple of flashlights so they split up to round up some more searchers.

It was dark by the time they set out again. Kramer and Brad left together headed east. Hardly anyone headed out this direction, it was far more densely wooded and covered with poison oak. Brad and

Kramer knew this yet plunged in anyway.

"Do you know what poison oak looks like?" Brad could hear a little uncertainty in Kramer's voice.

"No, but I bet we will by tomorrow."

"Very funny."

Right then Brad saw something move in the trail in front of them. Both flashlights shot up the trail sweeping from side to side.

"Jared... Jared is that you?" For some reason Brad was frightened. He hadn't been scared like this since he went to the Scare Mare in eighth grade. His stomach tightened up and goose bumps popped up and down his legs. That's when he heard it again. The whispering from last night. This time he didn't think it was kids. He was wondering if some counselors were playing a prank on him.

"Do you hear that Kramer?" he whispered.

"Yeah," Kramer said aloud. "Its kind of creepy."

Brad finally shook off the willies and headed up the trail. The path they followed was more or less some smashed down weeds that wound through the woods. Brad and Kramer had to duck tree branches, fight their way through thorny bushes, and step over swampy holes and small ditches all along the 'trail'. The later it got and the farther away from camp, the smaller the chances were they would find Jared tonight. There was no way they were going to give up the search. One of his kids was not at home and Brad was determined to find him. Images kept popping into his mind of Jared laying face down in the river some where, or pulling himself up a steep embankment that he had just rolled down and broke his leg, or them finding his body mauled by a bear. The images tormented him until he began to pray. He started praying that they would find Jared, then prayed that God's will be done, and when he finished , for some odd reason, he was praying for Pastor Knoll. It gave him a strange sense of peace however, to be praying for someone who wasn't even here. Who wasn't involved in this ordeal.

"Isn't God great." Brad blurted out of no where.

"Brad?"

"Jared?"

Kramer and Brad started swinging their lights around wildly until Kramer spotted a boy about twenty feet to the right of them. It was

Jared. He was blinking and rubbing his eyes from the light when Brad rushed him and wrapped his arms around the boy's body in a huge bear hug.

"Now I know what the shepherd felt like in Jesus' parable."

"I am so glad you guys found me. I thought I was going to die. How come you didn't answer me earlier when I called?"

"We didn't hear you yell." Kramer said.

"It was a while ago. Right when the sun went down, I heard you guys whispering so I yelled for you. You didn't hear me?"

"We were still at the camp then, Jared. Anyway lets head back and get you some food. I bet you're hungry." Brad took off his jacket and gave it to Jared. "I bet you're cold too."

"Freezing."

Kramer radioed back to camp on his walkie-talkie. Jenny said they saved them some food and had plenty of hot chocolate. Just hearing that seemed to warm Jared up a bit. He started asking what they had for supper, and what it tasted like. Then the tears came, streaming down his cheeks.

"I'm sorry Brad. I'm so sorry. I promise I will never do anything like this again. I know God kept me safe for a reason. I'm sorry."

"I'm just glad you're safe. Where did you go?"

Just then, the whispering started again. Brad and Kramer shined their lights in the bushes, but didn't say anything this time. They didn't see anything so they continued forward, toward the camp.

"That's what I heard" whispered Jared. "I thought that was you."

Brad didn't know what to think. In a way, he hoped it was some kids playing a joke on them, but for their sakes, he hoped it wasn't. He knew now it wasn't a counselor, they wouldn't have done that to Jared, but another kid might.

Changing the subject Brad asked Jared again, "Where did you go?"

"I tried beating you guys home from the devotion this morning, and I guess I just got lost."

"But we were on the opposite side of camp this morning."

"We were?"

"Yeah, are you sure that's when you went off?" Brad asked perplexed.

"Yeah. That's weird I ended up all the way over here then."

They could see the lights of the camp and when they broke out of the bush, people were everywhere waiting for them. Brad rushed Jared to the kitchen and got him food. He was starting to itch and wanted to get in the shower. Jenny came up behind him and whispered in his ear. "Two down eleven more to go."

Chapter 5

"Can I get you something to drink?....Sir?"

James looked up surprised to see the smiling face was addressing him.

"Uh, sure, how 'bout a ginger ale."

"Alright, in the can or in a cup?"

"Cup please."

As the young woman began pouring James' soda his mind floated back to where it was just moments before. It had been a wonderful vacation. Hannah's parent's anniversary was beautiful, and for all his nervousness, it was great to see some familiar faces. He had even gone to breakfast with his father and had an in depth, and long overdue talk. He finally told his dad why he needed to leave. James' father, Leonard, had been hurt deeply when his son and young family moved away fifteen years ago. He had planned on his son taking over the church he had started, and felt like it was a personal rejection against him when his son took the church in Lendel instead. James had tried to explain that he felt like God was moving them out of California, and he knew he couldn't raise his two sons in San Diego. His dad didn't hear it though. He didn't see God working at the time either. All he saw was his son walking out on the ministry they had worked so hard to build, turning his back on 750 people who not only expected, but wanted him to take over as Pastor of the church. All of them, including his father felt like he had betrayed them, so in the last fifteen years this was the first trip they had made back to San Diego. Time heals. Leonard actually told his son how proud he was of him. The tears started to fall as he asked for his son's forgiveness, and James' tears began when his dad told him he knew that it was God's will also. He said he admired James, that it took a strong man to leave all he had and follow God to a little town in the middle of nowhere, and that it was obvious God had rewarded him. James didn't know at the time, but this would be one of the most important breakthroughs of his life. In the coming months, he would need his father's wisdom more than he could have ever imagined.

James' vacation had been wonderful, but he was ready to get back to work. He was so anxious for their plane to land, and to head to the satellite parking where their car was waiting for them. He looked at his wife sleeping beside him, she always looked so peaceful when she slept. He often wondered what she was dreaming about. Knowing her it would be something wonderful. If it wasn't, she could make it sound that way. She had that gift. Hannah could take the most mundane story or event, and tell it in a way that would keep your attention riveted on her every word. She was so descriptive, she painted with her words, and every story was a new masterpiece. Whoever said, "I think that I shall never see, a poem as lovely as a tree" had never heard his wife tell a story. He tried to imagine how things looked to her, if everything seemed like an event, going to the store, brushing her teeth, cooking macaroni and cheese. He had decided long ago that his wife appreciated life's simple pleasures more than he ever would, or could, and that made him love her even more.

He could feel the plane start to descend and saw Jason jerk from his nap and look around nervously. James started to laugh.

"Scare you a bit Jace?"

"I thought we might be going down."

"We are, but safely. Are you glad to be back?"

"Kinda, I missed Jackson a bit and, well, Cass too. But I already miss the ocean."

"You always will. I still do. But I missed the mountains, when we were there so I guess its all relative."

James couldn't believe how excited he was to get back. He felt a sense of urgency as he rushed the family off the plane and to the luggage terminal. He was picturing the deacon's faces when he told them he no longer wanted a salary. Hannah and him had discussed it over vacation and decided since her royalty checks were coming in so often and so large he no longer needed the salary. He would ask them to give half of it to the institute for scholarships, and use the other half to give Brad a much needed raise and a raise to Mark. He could hear their excitement and surprise when he told them Hannah had been writing books under a pen name, and they would rather give his salary to things that really needed it. He planned on telling them that at the deacons meeting Saturday morning. He didn't want them to tell anyone though. He didn't want Brad or Mark to feel like they owed him anything, and he didn't want any recognition for the scholarships, he just wanted to help.

Piling off the shuttle, they made their way to G-13 where they had left their car. It looked so lonely. When they had left, there had been cars all around and now it was the only car in the whole parking lot except for an old pickup. James loaded all their stuff in and headed for home. He would have to hurry and unpack so he could make it back to the church to meet the kids coming back from camp. They were coming in around 3:30. He had talked to Brad yesterday, and he had told him. He had also talked to Mark last Sunday afternoon, and strangely enough that was the only person he had talked to from Lendel. Jerry hadn't called, and he thought for sure he would have after the all-star game. Adam hadn't called about their bid on the house they wanted. Bill hadn't called, Ben hadn't called, neither had Steve. That was surprising. Again the urgency overcame James, pressing his foot firmer against the peddle.

Hannah broke the silence. "It doesn't seem like we were driving through here only ten days ago. It seems like a month."

"Yes it does…" James voice trailed off. It did seem like a long time ago since they were winding through these mountain roads. Every curve felt so familiar, every little farm was like a breath of fresh air, or an old smiling face welcoming them home.

They topped the final crest and plunged down quickly toward their small community. James checked the clock on the dash it was

2:45. Hannah had been asking since they got off the plane if they could drive over Skyline Drive before they went to their house. He would be cutting it close, but he decided to go over it anyway. He would rather see Hannah's smile and be a few minutes late, than let his wife down to be there early. He didn't have to be there at 3:30 anyway, they probably wouldn't get in from camp until 4:00, maybe later. James made a left turn onto Peak and followed it toward Skyline Drive. He felt Hannah squeeze his hand, and that was all the thanks he needed.

* * * *

Out of breath, Brad was headed back to camp, following the path they had found two nights earlier. It had lead back to a cave, with a small entrance. There was room for four medium sized men to stand completely inside. What was left of a fire, was smoldering underneath a small rock overhang that doubled as a shelf for some strange looking dolls. There was writing on the walls, but not the usual 'Sam wuz here', but deep writing. Some was written in another language, some was copied from the Bible, and some so blasphemous and perverted it physically hurt your eyes to read. When they had first came up on the cave they were searching for a boyfriend-girlfriend couple that had sneaked out after curfew. Every hair on Brad's neck had stood on end. He could feel the evil that used this as their dwelling and the whispering they had been hearing was almost at a deafening pitch, yet still not understandable, to him or the other two counselors with him. That night both of the counselors had left camp sick including Kramer who was rushed to the Emergency Room. Brad had gone back up this morning more out of curiosity than anything else. As he looked at the walls for the last time, something caught his eye. It was in large spray paint print on the back wall. "From whence cometh wars and fightings among you." *That's in James I think.* Brad was trying to remember if that had been there the other night. He didn't think so. Suddenly his heart skipped a beat. Someone was in the cave with him. He whipped around quickly but there was no one. There wasn't room enough to hide, but Brad knew someone or something was in the cave. He burst out the cave door, running full steam towards the camp, pausing just long enough to scratch his poison oak rash. He didn't look over his shoulder, he never thought of going back, right now all he wanted to see was their bus packed and loaded, and Jenny waiting in the doorway.

He burst through the vegetation and into the middle of the camp. He looked around to see only their bus on the grounds. It was loaded and Jenny was standing on its stairs. He sprinted with the last bit of energy he had across the camp grounds to the bus.

"What's a matter? You look like you've seen a ghost." Jenny said.

"Nothing. Lets go. I'll tell you about it on the way home. Where is everybody?"

"Almost everyone went home an hour ago. You were gone for a long time."

"I was?" Brad was confused as he tried starting the engine. *Just like in the movies.* Second try, still no luck. Fear had its hands wrapped around Brad's throat and with every turn of the key, they squeezed a little tighter. Finally, the engine caught fire and roared to life. Brad looked in the rear view mirror at the kids sitting behind him. None of them seemed to notice the bus hadn't started at first and were completely oblivious to the hellish experience Brad had been going through. With every mile of pavement the tires put between them and the camp, Brads fear was that much removed from his heart. He had related the whole story to Jenny by the time they reached Denver.

"Who do you think it was?"

"I don't know that it was a who."

"What do you mean?"

"I mean, I think SOMETHING was there. Do you remember when Pastor Knoll was preaching about spiritual warfare and he said the closer you get to where God wants you the harder Satan attacks. We were making some real breakthroughs with a lot of these kids and I think someone didn't want it to happen. The scarier alternative is that…well I don't know."

"What? Tell me."

"Well at times I felt like the whispering almost sounded like laughing. Like something was making fun of us for something, or was laughing because they knew something we didn't. It was like they had some inside information, and all the things we were teaching and striving for would be worthless to us, to me, if we knew what they knew. I don't know for sure but it seemed like they were after Kramer and me in specific. I am a little nervous to get back to Lendel. I keep thinking something might have happened. I don't know though, I could just be scared. Other than that how do you think camp went?"

Jenny thought it was good, that was obvious from the start. By the time she finished her case, Brad had to agree. The kids, especially the 8th graders, had grown more than he would have ever imagined. They grew closer to each other, to him, and most importantly to God. They had such in-depth talks and even he benefitted from the unique insight some of the kids brought to their discussions. But nothing stuck out in his mind more than the morning by Turkey Creek and the Rocky Mountain Sunrise. You could tell an immediate difference in the lives of the kids who had hiked up there that morning, and it was also a lasting difference. It was something difficult to explain, like they finally had a realization of God and his power. Almost like Moses on Mt. Sinai, it was that real to the kids, and that life altering. You could even see a glow on their faces that radiated from deep inside their hearts. Adam glanced at the radio to see what time it was. 8:00. He knew that wasn't right.

"Does anyone have a watch?"

"Yes" replied 20 voices more or less in unison.

"?Que hora es?" Brad asked in his limited, and by now familiar, Spanish.

"3:45,3:47,3:40"

Well they were already late but at least they were only 20 miles from Lendel. He was excited to see Pastor Knoll and he couldn't wait to tell him about camp. Knowing Pastor Knoll, he wouldn't have to either. James would ask him about it right away. He was the perfect pastor, and the father Brad never had.

* * * *

Jerry hung up the phone and mumbled something as he passed by Pam to the den.

"What did you say honey?"

"Nothing!" Jerry snapped. "Where's my laptop?"

"Probably in the car where you left it."

"Great. I told you to make Rachael take her car to Colorado Springs to that concert, now she has my laptop."

"Everybody couldn't fit in her car, and I didn't leave YOUR laptop in YOUR car." Pam fired back.

Jerry slammed the door and Pam could hear him mumbling. Jerry had been mumbling a lot the past week or so. His mood swings had been from one extreme to the other. She had never seen him so excited as when they signed the contracts for the rental houses, and she had never, never seen him as angry as he was last Tuesday night when she said she still wasn't convinced the Pastor was stealing. That's actually when the mumbling began. After she said that, he began talking so fast and so furious it wasn't understandable. She thought she could hear words but never could quite make sense of them. Since then, it had gotten more frequent and at times quite loud. She had thought about making him an appointment with a psychiatrist but knew he would just go crazy over that. He had closed his shop early three times this week, and didn't open it at all today. When he wasn't mumbling he was on the phone or heading to Bill or Adam's to discuss whatever it was they discussed.

Behind the closed door, Jerry was nervous. The paranoia that had gripped his life was spilling into every aspect of his life. He had even accused Pam of having an affair with Phillip. *Why does she stick with me?* Jerry had been questioning himself a lot more lately.

The deacons had voted him Speaker at their meeting two nights ago. How ironic, the more confidence others were placing in him, the less confident he felt. It was an honor and he felt like Bill should have been the Speaker, but they all agreed Jerry was probably the best man for the job. Even Phillip, who vehemently disagreed with the entire concept of the Speaker, said Jerry was probably the most qualified. At the time Jerry wondered what his motives had been, but later took it as a compliment. He did see Phillip's side, he himself had often been opposed to changing the constitution, which they had done, without the Pastor being present, but this was an act of desperation. There had to be some chain of command. This had never been more evident than last Sunday night's business meeting. The Deacons and Trustees had met along with Mark, who was the only staff member in Lendel, to discuss the situation. Jerry, Bill, Hank, Jack, and Adam had met before the meeting to pray. They had been meeting every night to pray and Adam would usually give a little encouragement talk to the group. Jerry still couldn't believe how badly he had misjudged Adam.

The meeting started good, but quickly took a turn for the worse. Phillip initiated the defiance by refusing to let Bill say anything about the pastor without first saying 'alleged' or 'allegations' or 'we have heard'. Bob Grant quickly stood with him refusing to hear anything negative about Pastor James. This had personally hurt Jerry, but it got worse. Ben was a little uneasy about the situation and Hank who had seemed so convinced began to waiver. Jerry had a burst of courage and decided to jump in:

"I hadn't planned on saying anything tonight but I felt something tugging on me to stand and talk and it's not Bill, if you know what I mean. I too had doubts at first, but I have seen so much first hand, I know he is stealing. Right now, that is the least of my worries. That's just the material part. My deeper worry is what he has been doing to this church. Look at us, we are supposed to be the spiritual leaders and here we are at each other's throats. Not only that, but he has completely lost touch with the direction of this church. He is spending so much of the church's time and money on that institute and nobody wanted it but him."

"Wait a minute." It was Phillip again. "We voted on that institute. It was a way for area kids to go to Bible college cheaply, and church kids could go for free."

"We didn't really vote on building it, we just approved the plans the Pastor had already began. Does the Pastor have a corner on God's leadership? Is he the only one God can talk to? No. God speaks through his people, not through one man. I don't think James understands that anymore. His ego is out of control, Jason is out of control, and my wife says he makes her feel uncomfortable."

"That's enough." Bob stood to his feet glaring at Jerry. "I don't want to hear another word from you Jerry. You're supposed to be a leader, someone I looked up to, and here you are lying, and gossiping, completely destroying a man who isn't even here. And if you say one more bad thing about Jace…just make sure you know what you are talking about."

Bill Peters stood up then and moved that they close the business meeting until a later date and that they vote on a moderator. Ben Humphreys was their unanimous choice.

The men broke up and went their ways except for Mark Nelson the Music Minister. He stayed behind with Bill and as Jerry was walking up the stairs he looked back to see Adam had joined them. He wondered where Adam had come from, but then hurried off to catch Bob.

"Bob…Bob." Jerry came up behind him and grabbed his arm. Bob just pulled away.

"Don't talk to me right now Jerry."

Jerry didn't. He respected Bob enough to leave him his privacy, but he was hurt. Bob and Jerry had been best friends since the second grade, when they had adjoining desks in Ms. Coffman's class. Bob had been there when Jerry's voice changed, for his first date, first kiss, and he was the first person he told of his engagement to Pam. When Bob got hired right out of high school at the mill, Jerry had showed his support even though Bob's parents were disappointed. Jerry and Pam had planned Bob's graduation party three years ago when he finally graduated from tech school. Pam had consoled Phyllis, and Jerry, Bob when their first child was still born. They had been through so much together and now Bob didn't even want to talk to him. Jerry started reassuring himself. *He'll come around. Once he gets more information, he'll come around.*

After this meeting, the deacons began talking about redefining their role in the church and the first phase of that was electing the Speaker. Jerry had told Pam, but her response wasn't what he expected. She told him she was disappointed he had gone along with all this. She also asked if he had prayed about it. That stung him. Had he prayed about it? What did she think he was doing every night with Adam and Bill? He had prayed more these last two weeks than any time in his life. Had he prayed about it? Did she think he was that bad of a man? Of course he had prayed, and he felt like this is what they should be doing. Pam was just jealous. She was jealous about the time he was spending at church, at Adam and Bill's, and she was upset about the money they invested with Adam in Valley Rentals. She didn't seem to appreciate his concern for the church anymore. At least the Deacons did. *She'll see soon enough*, he told himself.

Jerry's frustration was growing looking for his Rockies polo shirt. He didn't want to be late for their meeting tonight and he just knew Pam probably hid it from him. His anger was boiling over with every door he pulled open and every drawer he dug through.

"Where's my Rockies Shirt?!!!!"

* * * *

James pulled up to the church and was surprised to see several cars already there. He saw Jerry and Pam's car, Phillip's Suburban, Bill's truck, and Jack's truck. *I bet they're waiting for the kids.* James shook his head. *Great guys.* He opened the doors and headed toward his office. The lights were all off in the hallway, and the sun lowering in the sky was casting dark shadows in the church. James headed down the hall towards his office glancing in Mark's office as he passed by the door. Mark and Adam were seated across from one another talking. *He's here late,* James thought. He didn't even realize he hadn't seen Adam's car out front. James tried opening his office but it was locked. He didn't remember locking the door when he had left. He fumbled with his keys in the knob from the shadows on the door. Opening up the door an envelope fell on the floor. It was addressed to Pastor Knoll. He took the envelope and set it on his desk. He would look at it after Brad got back with the kids.

James was so proud of Brad. He could remember the first Sunday Robert had brought him to church. Brad came over and had lunch with them after the services. He was so quiet, but polite for a 12 year old. Four weeks later, he got saved and his mother came to see him get baptized. One year later both his mother and two older sisters were saved and baptized. He could remember how excited both Brad and Robert were. They had prayed twice a day for them, until they all three were saved, and had thanked the Lord every day since. Both of his sisters had married into the ministry and Brad had gone on to be the first graduating class from Mountain View Bible Institute. He got hired on right after school as the Youth Pastor and their Youth Pastor had moved to full time music (he later left the church for an opportunity in St. Louis). Brads father had died of a drug overdose when Brad was three years old. His mother had struggled financially, but somehow managed to get her degree in nursing and got hired on by Lendel's Caring Sisters Hospital. The Youth had grown quite a bit since Brad was hired and last year six of his seniors stayed to attend the institute.

The Institute had also been a blessing. From the moment it was dreamed up the intent had been for area kids to have a way to attend Bible college affordably. Every kid that attended from their church automatically went for free, and with the help of his salary, hopefully a few more from the area could go for free also. The school had grown by leaps and bounds and two years ago finally achieved full accreditation. It was his dream and the dream of the deacons to make it a free Bible college but to a limited number of kids, maybe 800 total.

James looked out the window eagerly awaiting the bus and saw Rachael's car pull up. Pam stepped out and James remembered the concert tonight. *I bet Rachael has Jerry's car. Pam must be pretty eager to see Gerry,* James thought. James looked down at his desk and saw the letter again. *Pastor Knoll. Maybe I should go ahead and read it now.* James took out his letter opener and carefully opened one end of the envelope. He held it in his right hand and softly tapped his wrists together, squeezing the edges so the letter slid out neatly. The letter came out and James opened it up to see a picture right in the middle. It was a picture of Adam and Candy Lesik, a few years younger, standing on either side of a middle aged man with their arms around him. He was tall and thin and wore a nice black suit. James was searching his brain to see if he knew this man, but couldn't place him if his life depended on it. He finally set the picture down, giving up on recalling this man's face, and decided to read the letter.

Dear Pastor Knoll,

My name is Jensen Andrews. I am the man in the picture I sent to you. I was the Pastor of the Friendship Bible Church in

Buckley, Minnesota for 18 years. Our church grew from 10 people meeting in our living room to 400 members in 12 years. Adam and Candy came to our congregation at about that time. I remember because right away they were wanting to get involved. It was exciting to me to see a young couple, just married wanting to serve the Lord. I had them start a singles ministry and before long, they had 150 single adults in their class. It was amazing. Then the trouble started. They began questioning my motives for decisions I was making, questioning how money was being spent, questioning my ability to pastor, my credibility. They began making flip remarks about me being a false teacher, having sexual indiscretions, about my children's behavior, and pretty soon, these 'non-accusing' comments began to stick. People started to believe them, and it all began to snowball. I began thinking about resigning and talked to many Pastor friends who advised me to stick it out and see it through. I tried. Finally, it came to the point where the Deacon Board was going to ask me to resign. These were some of my closest friends. They had been convinced that I was evil, that I was a dictator trying to reign supreme over every aspect of their lives, that I was leading them down the pathway of destruction. They had been convinced that I was no longer following God, and they began to create their own distorted view of God, a God that had no definitive right and wrong, a God without absolutes, a God that catered to however men felt, not what was true. They were being led astray by Adam in their prayer meetings of all places. His prayers were manipulative and played purely off the emotion, making people feel like they were in Gods will. He gave his devotions without any type of biblical input but just whatever he 'felt' like God wanted him to say. I am reminded of Timothy when Paul warned him of men having a form of godliness, but denying the power thereof. The power comes from the Word of God, not from the feelings of men, or the thoughts of their minds.

Anyway, they ended up asking me to resign, which I did thinking then I might be left alone and at least spared some of my reputation. I knew I could never minister in this area again, but maybe somewhere else. I wasn't left alone. I was charged with embezzlement and fraud, neither charge stuck however. Still this wasn't enough. My wife began receiving love letters I had supposedly written a young lady in the church. She didn't believe them of course, at first, but then she got a picture taped to her windshield of me and another woman kissing. It wasn't real it had been superimposed somehow, I still don't know who the woman was or how they did it, but that was the last straw. She left me just over four years ago. I haven't seen my children or her in over two.

I am not writing you for pity, but to warn you. The Lesiks moved two weeks to the day my wife left. I have tried to track them down ever since. I am sorry it took me this long to let you know. I enclosed a picture in case you were doubting it was the same Lesiks. Be careful, my brother, be careful.

In Christ's Loving Care,
Jensen

Chapter 6

Brad pulled the bus over next to the Lendel city limits sign. The kids all piled off wondering if they were having engine trouble or a blown tire. As the last kid stepped off Brad had them all join hands around the sign and pray for their town and community. Gerry started first. She had been sick a lot at camp and after the Sunrise Service barely was able to keep any food down, but she hadn't let that discourage her. She had grown a lot and made some important decisions. Never missing a chapel or devotion, she won a newly invented award, The Trooper. Her prayer came from her lips so pure and so honest several kids started to cry. Next was Patrick. He had just recently gotten saved and though he didn't know all the Christian lingo it was the sweetest prayer Brad had ever heard. These kids were pouring out their hearts and concern for their community, for their friends. Brad wished the entire congregation could hear these kids pray. It was all so honest, it wasn't like a speech or something preconceived but it was truly talking with God, truly praising God, and true thanksgiving. *No wonder Jesus said suffer the children unto me,* Brad thought, *they really know Him.* Brad finally felt the squeeze on his hand and he closed in prayer. With the last Amen, they all exchanged hugs and loaded onto the bus to head for the church.

The whole trip home Brad had been thinking how good this camp had been for the kids. His attitude had suddenly changed. How good it had been for him. He needed this, the fire that had burned inside him for lost souls when he was a teenager praying for his mother, was beginning to grow again. He thanked God for the kids and his wife.

Sliding in close to the curb, Brad decided to go up on it a little and give the kids a bit of a bounce. Angela was standing up and landed in Patrick's lap. All the kids roared with laughter, they had been a pegged couple since the beginning of the trip and neither had the guts to talk to the other. *A perfect ending* Brad thought.

The church's parking lot looked like an airport terminal, with luggage and parents and kids, hugging everywhere you turned. Brad laughed and put his and Jenny's luggage into their trunk. It wouldn't be too much longer until he'd be putting in a stroller as well. He was getting anxious for the baby to be born. They had wanted it to wait until after Jr. High camp, so now they were ready. Sometimes he wished they knew what it was but Jenny had convinced him, not with the first. Brad had even said he wouldn't tell her but she still wouldn't agree.

"I'm going to talk to the Pastor for a minute Jenny."

"Yeah, right. More like an hour. Do you mind if I go on home and start unpacking and you can just catch a ride home with him?"

"That's fine. I love you." Brad said and moved to give Jenny a quick kiss on the lips. Jenny pulled back.

"Are you trying to get rid of me?"

"No…I thought…you said."

"Just kidding." And Jenny gave him a peck and a hug. "See you at home."

"See ya." Brad shook his head when Jenny was out of sight. He snickered a little bit, he could never understand her. Especially now that she was pregnant, but that made him love her all the more.

The knock on the door startled James and he turned the letter he was reading face down on his desk.

"Come in." It was Brad, "Hi, Brad." James said, getting up from his chair and giving Brad a hug. "How was camp?"

"Fantastic, how was your trip?"

"It was good. Have a seat, I want to hear all about camp first. Did Frankie do a good job as the speaker?"

Another knock on the door interrupted Brad before he began.

James didn't even have a chance to say "come in" before Jerry went ahead and stepped in.

"Jerry, good to see you." Pastor Knoll said blissfully.

"Yeah, uh, James, could we speak to you, uh, in private." Jerry was looking at the floor the whole time and James knew something was bothering him.

He hadn't seen Oscar when he got home so maybe he had run away or something. He'd have to give Jerry a hard time if that was the case.

"Sure Jerry. Who's we?"

"Just the deacons and a couple of other guys."

"Alright. Okay if Brad comes along? Maybe he can fill us in on camp."

"Uh, I'd rather not. It's uh, kind of private." Jerry then looked up at Brad. "It might take us a while so you should probably go on home."

"That's alright" Brad said. "Jenny already left, and I want to talk to the Pastor anyway."

"Suit yourself." With that, Jerry stretched his hand to the door as a cue for the pastor to exit. James went out and waited for Jerry to pass him and lead him to where they were going.

It's not Oscar, James thought, *and if some one had died, they would have called. Maybe somebody messed up morally, man I hope not.*

They reached the bottom of the stairs and James saw the tables set up in a square. All the deacons were there along with Mark, Adam and Steve. Both Steve and Phillip looked as though they had been crying, but Phillip wouldn't look at him as he walked in.

"Have a seat." Jerry said, and pulled out a chair facing all the men.

James sat down and Jerry walked around the table to take his place at the head. Bill sat on his left hand side and Adam on his right. James started to feel sick. He was recalling the letter, at first he hadn't believed it, he thought it was some crack-pot wanting to inflict some damage on the Lesiks, but now, strangely enough, he could see Adam and Candy doing that.

"So, fellas, what did you want to talk about?"

"We didn't actually want ta talk." Jack said with a smirk. "We wanted to ask."

"So ask." James said holding his palms up and spreading his arms as a sign he had nothing to hide.

"We have reason to believe..."Jerry started but was interrupted by Phillip getting up and walking out.

"Let him go." Adam said to Jerry.

Jerry looked thrown for a minute then regained his composure, "We have reason to believe you have been stealing from the church. Spiritually and monetarily."

Those words hit James like a slap in the face. He was completely unprepared for this type of accusation. And what did Jerry mean stealing spiritually? James could feel the blank stare on his face and wondered if his mouth was open.

"What are you talking about?"

It was silent and James looked at each man individually. Bill and Jerry looked away, Mark looked down, Steve was shaking his head with tears streaming down his face, Jack was smiling, and Adam just stared back. Childishly, James stared at him and told himself don't look away first. Adam wouldn't blink, wouldn't dart his eyes, and wouldn't shift his body, nothing. Finally, Jerry broke the uncomfortable silence.

"There is money missing from the Missions Account. There are low offerings. There is the fact that no one feels like they can come to you for anything. The fact that you feel you are the only one God can speak to. I'm personally tired of the way you look at Pam, and you tried bribing me with tickets you bought with money you stole from me. I ask you, what are YOU talking about?"

Steve got up this time and left. James had been counting him as an ally and now he was pretty much on his own. Suddenly an unexplained peace came over him, he knew he wasn't alone, he could remember all his trips to Skyline Drive and Psalm 23 began going over and over in his mind. "Yea, though I walk through the valley of the shadow of death I will fear no evil, for thou art with me, thy rod and thy staff comfort me."

He defended himself as much as he could but every time he started to make some progress Adam would but in and thwart his advances. It was like two Generals commanding their troops. Every once in a while he could feel an ambush being set and he would back away. After two hours, the men finally decided to call it a night. James saw a difference in Jerry from the beginning to now, and felt he was probably more confused now than ever. James suggested they meet tomorrow night and he would bring all his financial records and have Steve bring all the church's for the men to look them over. This seemed to satisfy the group and brought up some guilt feelings in their lives. Except Jack and Adam, they remained unconvinced. Jerry however was torn. The flag of Paranoia was slowly lowering and the flag of Hope was being prepared to raise.

James headed up the stairs to see Brad waiting there. Jerry and Jack had gone home but Mark, Bill and Adam stayed behind. They were downstairs praying, or talking, or conniving. James wished he hadn't thought that, but he had. He was upset, and hurt, the peace he felt earlier was still there but the human side of him felt completely crushed. How could they have ever thought he was stealing. He had told them his wife was writing under a pen name and that he had planned to give his salary back to the church, and still there was doubt. It hurt. James then thought how Jesus must have felt when Judas betrayed him. He had never really thought of it that way before. Jesus would have felt pity, and anger, but most of all sorrow. He had loved these men as Jesus loved his disciples, and they had turned on him.

"Are you alright?" Brad asked, "You look sad."

"I am Brad. Do you have a few minutes?"

"Sure."

They moved to James' office and Brad took a seat. James sat in the chair right next to him rather than behind the desk. James took a deep breath and ran his hands through his hair locking his fingers on the back of his head and his elbows pointed at Brad.

"They think I'm stealing." He said quietly.

"What?! Who?!"

"Yeah, Jerry said there was money missing from the mission's account. $15,000."

"Isn't that how much we approved to give to the Institute at the last business meeting?"

"Yes, but apparently no one remembers. Well, I don't know, maybe the trustees do. I guess I should call them for our meeting tomorrow night. They have some other issues besides that, but you can hear all of them tomorrow night. Oh, I guess I should ask you to come first. It's at 6:00."

"I'll be there. I just can't believe it. I really don't know what to say. I bet Jack was enjoying it. He's probably behind it all, fudging the numbers. I should just go punch him."

James laughed hollowly. "That's not necessary. It'll work out. Now tell me about camp."

Brad went on to tell Pastor Knoll all about camp, from the Rocky Mountain Sunrise to the feeling in the cave. Everything except the writing on the wall. After he finished, they prayed for the kids and for tomorrow night and as always James gave Brad a passage of Scripture for them to study and a couple verses to memorize.

On the way home, James thought about heading up Skyline Drive, but decided against it. He was feeling a little betrayed and he could hear a part of him saying *You don't deserve this. You've done so much for these people and look how they repay you. You were even going to give up your salary,* but then the words of Jesus would flood his mind "Whosoever will come after me, let him deny himself, and take up his cross, and follow me." "Forgive them Father for they know not what they do." Never in his forty-one years as a Christian had those words been so clear and understandable to him. They didn't know what they were doing. They were doing what they thought was best for the church. They were doing what they thought was right. How could he blame them, but after tomorrow night it would all be okay. He'd show them his finances, his wife's checks and it would all be back to normal. All the stuff about him stealing from them spiritually, that was probably just created because of what they thought was going on. If someone was stealing from the offering, what would keep them from lying from the pulpit? Once he proved he wasn't stealing, everything else would go away.

Hannah was waiting by the door when he got home.

"Where've you been? I was worried."

"I had a deacon's meeting tonight."

“You did?” Hannah looked confused.

“Yeah, kinda spur of the moment thing, I guess.”

“Oh. Did it go good?”

“Alright.” James said shrugging his shoulders.

He had decided against telling his wife everything right now. It would all be over tomorrow and he really didn’t want her to get upset over nothing. He’d just wait and tell her a little later, when it was all over with. Right now, however, he would go looking for their bank statements and call Steve.

* * * *

Jerry could hear his phone ringing as he opened the front door.

“Hello…No he isn’t, can I take a message?…Adam?…Yeah, I sure will…Bye.”

Jerry was a little glad he had missed Adam’s call. He needed to sort through some things in his mind. He was so confused. Maybe Pastor wasn’t stealing from them. He never really believed he had been stealing anyway, and his ‘ego’ hadn’t really showed up at their meeting, and if it had been a problem with him wouldn’t it have shown up then? No temper, no lying, he didn’t seem nervous, he wasn’t defensive. He had been calmly direct and straight forward. Maybe they had all gotten carried away.

He sneaked into the kitchen and came up behind Pam wrapping his arms around her waist, he squeezed gently, lifted her off the floor and twirled her around.

“Jerry Pattison, what are you doing?” Pam said in between laughs.

“I love you honey.”

“I love you too. What’s going on?”

“Nothing.”

“Nothing? Did you have your meeting tonight?”

“Yes.”

“How did it go?”

“Good. I don’t think the Pastor is stealing.”

“See. I told you.”

“Please don’t say that. It makes me wish he was when you get all cocky like that.” Pam could tell Jerry was serious and not joking.

"Fine. You don't have to get all upset over it though."

"I'm not upset, I just wish that...Oh never mind. Who was on the phone when I came in." Jerry already knew the answer he just wanted to get an excuse to leave.

"Adam. Now finish what you were saying."

"It isn't important. I'm going to call Adam back."

"Please don't Jerry. He'll just try to get you upset again."

"I can think for myself."

"Fine."

Pam watched Jerry walk to the den and saw their 'line in use' light come on. *He hadn't even said hi to Gerry, or asked how camp went, or even asked if she made it home.* What had happened to her husband? Jerry used to be the most caring man she knew. She had always felt he was so sensitive to Spiritual issues and seemed to always hear and obey the softest urging of the Holy Spirit. He used to spend hours with the girls, talking, taking them on dates, playing games. He used to take her out at least one night a week, they hadn't even really talked in ten days. Jerry used to read the Bible every morning. He would wake up an hour before everyone else and sneak out to his den to read the Bible and pray. Every once in a while she would get up just to watch him. He never knew it. She had even seen him cry reading the Bible. Pam hadn't even seen Jerry pick up the Bible, even for church, in at least six months. It seems when he began to neglect his time with the most important person in his life, Pam should have realized everyone else would follow suit. What had happened? Before Pam could answer that question, the light went off on the phone. She heard Jerry head down the hall, and the mumbling follow him all the way through the slam of their bedroom door.

* * * *

"So they actually thought Pastor was stealing?" Jenny asked.

"Yep. Even Jerry. That surprised me a little, I mean, I could definitely see Jack, probably Mark, and maybe even Bill, but no way Jerry. That completely blew me away. I hate Jack. He's probably the one who started it all. I could just hear him lying and making things up. I ought to call him."

"Now Brad. You might want to wait until you cool off. I know you and I know you will end up saying something you'll regret."

"I don't know. I think I can hold my cool longer than Jack, and maybe I could make him mad enough to get him to cuss me out or something. Someone needs to stand up to him and it looks like none of the deacons are going to. Mark definitely isn't, so I guess the buck gets passed to me. I can't just sit around and do nothing."

"At least wait until after your meeting tomorrow. See how things go, it might be better than you expect."

"Yeah you're right. At least tomorrow, we'll have some help with the trustees, and Steve, and hopefully Phillip won't run out this time. That kind of surprised me. First of all, I would think he might be on the other side of the equation, given how close he is to Bill, and secondly, he gave up so easily."

"You don't know what happened while we were away. He could have been fighting the whole time and just didn't want to deal with it anymore, or maybe he was embarrassed."

"Maybe. I do think they, no, I know they had a Deacon's meeting while everyone was gone. That makes me really mad at Mark too. He's been kind of a punk from day one and this just solidifies it. He doesn't have a heart for ministry, he just wants an 'easy' job where he makes decent money and gets complimented all the time. That's just what it is to him too. A job. You know what else?"

"What?" Jenny asked, truly curious.

"I think that all that whispering I heard at camp was about this. I think it was an orchestrated event, and I was being laughed at because they knew what would happen when we got back."

"I think your starting to blow it all out of proportion. James doesn't sound that upset, apparently, he thinks it will all be over tomorrow. Maybe you should take a lesson from his behavior."

"You didn't see his face Jenny. You didn't see the sadness and the hurt in his eyes. I have never seen him look like that before and I honestly wanted to see Jack suffer for what he has done to James. I don't think it will blow over. I think they will drum up more and more and more until James can't take it anymore. I mean think about it, if someone could make themselves believe James was stealing, they could make themselves believe anything. And they will."

Chapter 7

"Fine!" Jerry slammed the receiver down on the phone base.

He put his face in his hands and an angry growl ripped through his clinched teeth. He slammed both his fists on the desktop as he stood up, hoping in vain it would relieve some of the anger he was feeling. He could hear his daughter out front talking to a couple boys who had been getting quite a few items dry cleaned these last few weeks. Jerry had hired Rachael two weeks ago when her swimming lessons job at the pool ended. She would be starting school a week from Tuesday, so this was giving them a chance to spend a little time together before she got too busy with school and various activities. Jerry didn't care for either of the boys out front, and had let Rachael know on several occasions. Right now, the way he felt, their voices were about enough to drive him over the edge. He was moments from snapping and tossing both boys out onto the street, after he finished beating on them. Suddenly, he heard one of them whisper something to Rachael, and then heard her giggle. That was it, that was the straw that broke the camels back. He charged through the saloon doors that divided the customer area from the back, and turned the corner heading to the front counter. As soon as he turned, he realized there was no one in the store. Rachael wasn't there, the two boys weren't there, no one. He looked up at the clock, and was taken aback by what he saw. 5:25. He had been on the phone for an hour and a half, Rachael had probably left 15 minutes ago. So, who had he heard talking? He had definitely heard voices. He looked around the store and nobody was there, the front door was locked and he would have seen anyone go in the back. He looked down at his arm as he felt the goose bumps start to puff up and see the hairs stand on end. What had he heard? He remembered Bob's words just a little while ago:

"Your imagination is only matched by your ego." Maybe that's what it was, his imagination.

Bob had called around 4:00 this afternoon. He had apparently taken the day off work and had gone to Phillips to work themselves into a frenzy. Between Phillip, Brad Kramer and Bob, they could really get themselves angry, and that's how Bob called. Angry. Maybe at first he didn't sound angry, but Jerry knew that's what it was. He had tried to come in his sheep's clothing, pretending he was just concerned about Jerry, wanting to work things out with him, wanting to help him get things right with Pastor Knoll, when all the while Jerry knew he was just fishing for information, and when Jerry didn't give any he got angry. The deacons had decided that they could no longer have open discussions with several of the men in the church, because of loose tempers, and Bob would definitely be added to the list. He had even been so brash as to say:

"When I'm at the judgment seat, I'm just glad I won't have to say my name is Jerry Pattison. That would be my nightmare."

My nightmare Jerry scoffed at this statement. Jerry had just finished telling Bob about the nightmare he had been having. Jerry was sitting in the basement of the church with all the deacons there, and sitting at the head of the table was Satan. He would talk to the men for hours, telling them stories, and getting them motivated to do what he was about to ask, and no one could see he was the devil himself. He wasn't disguised, or an angel of light, just no one recognized him. Then midway through his dream he would have a moment of clarity and he would realize that Satan was the one talking to them. He would look around terrified, and one by one, he would see the other deacons realizing, he could tell by the terror on their faces. The odd thing was Phillip was never in any of the dreams. He had never really believed in dreams or prophecy or anything like that, but he thought maybe it was some kind of a premonition that James was a false prophet. Possibly even spiritually led, but not by good spirits. In fact, in some ways, these nightmares had hardened his position against James, and they seemed to be coming more frequent.

Bob, on the other hand, was completely convinced James had done nothing wrong. He hadn't really gone out and tried to win people over to his view point, but he had argued more than once with Jerry. Jerry was getting sick of it. Bob and Nancy had invited Jerry and Pam over for dinner last Sunday after church. Jerry and Pam agreed, realizing it might be a time for mending hurt feelings, but apparently, the Grants had other ideas. While Bob occupied Jerry in the living room with the Rockies game, Nancy cut Pam off from the rest of the troop and began hammering her about James. She was extremely thorough, she could have been a brainwashing agent in Hitler's Nazi regimen.

She completely changed Pam's mind, and all the way home Jerry had to listen to her singing James' praises, and questioning good men's agendas, such as Bill and Adam. Jerry was furious at Bob for this, and until today, he hadn't spoken to him.

Why did Bob call anyway? Jerry thought to himself. Then he remembered. It sickened him to think about how selfish Bob had become. He had actually called to see if the deacons would be willing to bring this matter before the entire church, and let the people decide what should happen. *How selfish can he be. We are trying our darndest to keep these kind of problems from the church body. We are trying to protect people from this kind of embarrassment. He just wants everyone else to suffer like we are having to or maybe he just wants the monkey off his back.* Jerry had told a few people about what was going on. He had visited some of the couples that were considered 'big tithers' because he was concerned about the way their money was being spent. He thought they had a right to know. Most of them were completely shocked, and one couple had even quit coming. He didn't want that to become the trend, he didn't want to lose people because of one man who would be out of there soon enough, so he toned down his visits a bit. He thought some of the people had a right to know, but he did not want it to come to the whole church for fear of a split.

Bob is so selfish and conniving. Conniving. That was probably the best word for him. He was the one who wrote the letter to the deacons. He was the one who, at the men's meeting, brought up the fact that he thought there had been a lot of sneaking around, which prompted a lot of questions; he was the one who said he would stand by James 100%; he was the one listening to Phillip and having meetings at his house. Bob was the one doing these things. Not Jerry.

Just then, Jerry heard the phone ring. He was already spooked and with his mind completely oblivious to his presence in his shop, the first ring made his muscles jump and jerk his breath into his lungs with one quick, loud, reaction. He looked around self-consciously, to make sure no one had seen him, then moved towards the phone, as graceful as possible, just in case someone outside could see him.

"Hello."

"Hi Jerry, it's Mark."

* * * *

Hannah passed by their bedroom with an armful of towels headed towards the bathroom. She could hear quiet sobbing coming from inside. She pushed the door open a bit and saw James sitting on their bed facing the window. His head hung in his hands and his shoulders were slumped, and his crying moved his entire body up and down softly. She stepped in the room quietly moving over to the bed. She sat down beside him, slid her arm around his shoulders, pulling him close to her. Tears were welling up in her eyes as she saw James heart breaking, and tears pouring down his face.

"Are you okay Honey?" Hannah knew he wasn't, she was just trying to get him to open up.

"What did I do? All I've ever wanted was to preach the Word and love the people."

"I know Honey." Hannah squeezed him tight. "I'm sorry."

"You know the thing that hurts the worst is that these were people I thought were close friends. How can Jerry believe I stole? How can he believe any of these things?" James voice broke, his crying was audible.

He slid off the bed and knelt on the floor, falling into the loving arms of his Father, giving all his problems over to God.

* * * *

Brad looked at his wife sitting in the passenger seat. He reached over and patted her tummy.

"You'll get um next time tiger." Brad said trying to cheer her up. But from the look she gave him, he knew it hadn't worked. "God knows when the baby is ready to meet us honey, and I'm sure it won't be much longer."

Jenny burst into tears. Brad rubbed her back softly. He wanted to say something but didn't know what might help. He had thought Jenny was having real labor pains today. She had been having Braxton Hick's for over a month now, but these contractions were totally different. He was a little disappointed when the doctor said "false alarm" but not nearly as disappointed as his wife. What could he say? He decided to pull over and hug her and comfort her as much as he could. He pulled the car over about a mile from their house at a little park some of the teenagers frequented. It's official name was Bagley Park, but was more commonly referred to as 'stoner park'. Unfastening his seat belt, he slid across the bench seat right next to Jenny and wrapped his arms around her. She buried her head in his chest and began sobbing. He was doing more for her without saying a word, than a million spoken words by a counselor or friend could ever do. He just needed to be there.

Brad had been holding Jenny, and even crying a bit himself and hadn't noticed the group of kids sitting on a picnic table about a 100 yards away. He hadn't noticed that they were smoking and drinking. He hadn't noticed they had been cussing and wrestling and a few couples were making out. He hadn't noticed any of this until the sunlight hit a shiny silver beer can and the reflection nearly blinded him. He squinted for a second and then the can moved to the mouth. Brad shook his head and squinted his eyes again. This time, however, it wasn't from the sun it was because of the mouth the beer was pouring into. It was Rachael Pattison's mouth. He saw her swallow the alcohol and wrinkle up her face obviously not enjoying the taste, but then the can moved to her mouth again and this time poured over her lips and down her throat, for much longer than it had the first time. He saw someone offer her a puff on whatever it was he was smoking, Brad couldn't quite tell from there, but at least Rachael refused that. As she lifted the can one more time, Brad whispered for Jenny to look. She also squinted through puffy, tear filled eyes.

"Huh" she gasped when her vision finally cleared and she was able to focus on

what Brad had been pointing at. "Is it…it can't be…I never would have thought… Rachael?"

"Man. What do we do hun? I mean do we say something to her, or call Jerry, or do we just leave it alone? What do you think? Should I say something?"

"No, don't say anything to her right now. Maybe later in private. I think we definitely ought to tell Jerry and Pam though."

"I don't think he'll believe me. I wish I had a camera."

"What? No way, that would be way too creepy."

"I know. I can't tell if I'm more worried, or more disappointed."

"I'm more worried. I'm not disappointed at all. What can you expect, I mean with all the stuff going on at church, and I know Jerry and Pam haven't been getting along to well lately, and you really haven't been as focused on the youth as you were just a little while ago--"

"--Honey I've had to do a lot of stuff because of the problems--"

"--I know, I know, I'm not blaming you, its just a combination of things. I feel sorry for her. She has to be uncomfortable around Jason, and now that he is dating Cassie, she really has no good friends to be hanging out with. Honestly, Cassie was a better influence on her, than she was on Cassie."

"Yeah, its sad. I think everybody is kind of overlooking the youth in this whole thing. Even me. We're taking them for granted, and this just proves it." Brad said pointing out the car window towards the kids.

Right then Rachael looked up to see Brad pointing directly at her. She dropped the can she was holding, startling the rest of the crowd. All heads turned toward her and Brad saw her say something to the group, excusing herself, then walk briskly to the other side of the park where her Super Beetle was parked. After she walked about 30 yards, she took one quick glance back over her shoulder and then broke out in a dead sprint to her car. Brad and Jenny watched awestruck, as she jumped in her car and flipped a quick U barely missing a speeding truck, and headed off at light speed toward her house. Brad and Jenny were speechless. They drove the rest of the way to their house in complete silence.

Brad opened the front door carrying all their luggage they had taken to the hospital. It was amazing to Brad how much stuff one pregnant woman needed. It made him laugh when he thought about his tiny Wal-Mart bag with everything he needed, even for an extended stay, sitting next to Jenny's giant cargo bag. He had joked with her about renting a U-Haul next time she decided to make a hospital run. Stumbling through the front door his shoulders slumped and he dropped all the bags right next to their front door. This had become the official spot for the baby bag, Jenny's over night bag and a miscellaneous bag ever since they got back from camp. Jenny had apologized all the way in about Brad having to carry all the bags and Brad was eating it up, continuing to make her feel guilty with his painful sound effects. As he dumped the bags, he saw their answering machine light flashing. Immediately he thought, Rachael had told Jerry and he was calling. Dreadfully he hit the play button, not wanting to talk to Jerry.

"You have two messages and one new message. Message one."

I wonder why they always use female voices for mechanical voices, and never males. Brad's mind was drifting as he listened to the two old messages for the fifteenth time in a week. For some reason they never erased these two messages. There was nothing important on them, no phone numbers, no reminders, they just always forgot to hit delete on the first one and laziness just prevented the second message from getting 86'd. *I wonder if it's the same for other countries, I bet not in India. I bet they have to have male voices, because they could never take instructions from a female.* That thought made Brad laugh.

"Message three."

"High Brad this is Mark, could you give me a call when you get in. Thanks."

Chapter 8

Pam heard tires screech and the ugly sound of metal crunching. She looked up from the sink, where she was washing the pizza pan that had just served them dinner, curiously hoping to see what happened. Her curiosity took on a sickening horror as she looked out the window to see a shiny pink VW Bug jammed underneath the back of a trash truck. The car's horn was sounding automatically, calling for an ambulance, or maybe announcing a death. The horn seemed to be louder than ever before, almost like a train whistle, and the sound was multiplying Pam's terror as she rushed out the door toward her daughters limp body still sitting in the drivers seat, her face inches from the back of the truck. The driver and his partner had already gone to the, now completely shattered drivers side window, and one was on the phone hopefully with 911. As Pam sprinted across the street she could hear one of the men talking softly to Rachael, and that gave her a little hope that she was still conscious. Finally reaching the car, Pam pushed the man away from the window and grabbed her daughter's hand. Rachel's eyes moved towards her mothers and she tried to turn her head to face her.

"Mom I'm sorry." She said so softly Pam had trouble hearing it.

"It's okay dear. It's okay. You're going to be fine. It will all be okay." Tears were streaming down Pam's cheeks and she hoped Rachael didn't see the fear in her eyes. She was praying and patting Rachael's hand trying to keep her from blacking out.

"I'm sorry." Rachael whispered and blacked out.

* * * *

Cars honked furiously as Jerry flew through the intersection of Collins and Orchard. He had been about a hundred feet away when the light turned red but he didn't slow down at all, narrowly missing his death disguised as a silver Tahoe. Pam had called him, completely hysterical, only ten minutes ago. The paramedics had taken Rachael to the hospital in Lendel and were going to see if they could get her stabilized. Jerry hadn't had any time to really think about the situation or his daughter, he had just reacted purely out of instinct.

His heart was pounding as he reached the receptionists desk. His fear was obvious as he asked where his daughter was, and Jerry felt like the receptionist was taking a long time on purpose. He couldn't help how rude he must have sounded but his anxiety was growing by the second. He finally got the information he needed and raced through the doors at the end of the hall straight back to the emergency room. The first thing he saw when he got to the waiting room was his wife sitting alone sobbing heavily.

"Pam." She turned her head and when her eyes met Jerry's she rushed to him and fell into his arms.

"Jerry, I'm so scared. You should have seen her. She looked so small and I felt so helpless. The doctors haven't said a word to me yet."

"It'll be okay Honey." But even as the words came out of Jerry's mouth, he didn't believe them. "She's in God's hands."

* * * *

"I'm outta here mom, see you after awhile."

"Wait a minute, where you going?"

"To Cassie's, remember? Dad said I could."

"Alright. What time are you coming home?"

"It won't be too late. Maybe 11:30."

"11:00. No later."

"Come on mom."

"10:30"

"Alright, alright, 11:00. Bye."

"Bye."

Hannah watched Jason shut the door behind him and head down their sidewalk to his truck parked by the curb. Watching him drive away the same feelings overtook her that did the first time she left him in the nursery, the first time James and her left him overnight at a babysitters, the first time he went to school, the first time he waited for the bus without mom or dad. Each time it felt like she was losing a part of him, she could never have back. It hadn't been quite the same with Robert, by the time he was going to school, they were still planning their family and Jason showed up when Robert was 10. She loved Robert just as much, and there was something special about the relationship between the oldest son and his parents, but Jason was their baby. As Robert grew, Hannah always knew that a lot of the things she would get to experience again, to cherish again, but now she only had memories. She would never get to brush her sons teeth, or put their little shoes on, or pour peroxide on a cut knee while patching the hole in his jeans. Just memories.

James came into the living room and stood beside his wife facing out the door.

"Jason leave?" He asked.

"Yeah he's going to Cassie's."

"Spending an awful lot of time over there isn't he."

Hannah smiled and turned around, wiping her face with the back of her hands hiding any trace of the tears that had fallen just moments ago.

"What's that?" She asked pointing to a small package James was holding in his hands.

"This?" James held the package in the air. "Oh this is just something a church in South Carolina sent me. They're looking for a Pastor, and J.R. Delvy, remember him from school, anyway, he told them to get in touch with us. He said we would probably know of someone, maybe graduating from the Institute that would be a good candidate. It's kind of a small church, about 120, but only 10 miles from the coast. I thought I might run this over to Dave and Julie's and see if they're interested. Wanna come along?"

"Sure, let me just grab my purse."

James headed out to the garage and started the car. He opened the garage door and backed the car out. He was listening to the Rockies game on the radio until he saw Hannah step out the front door. He shut off the radio and got out of the car. He walked briskly around to the passenger door and held it open for her like he always did. She smiled and thanked him and he hurried around to get in on his side.

They visited with Dave and Julie for about an hour before they left. They both seemed interested, but also expressed some concerns about moving so far away from their families. They did say they would pray about it though and that seemed to satisfy James.

"You were pretty excited when you were telling them about the church, James."

"Well yeah, it kind of reminds me of our church when we first came out here."

"Have you thought about leaving, maybe taking another church?"

"No, not right now. Well both of us have talked about when I retire, but not right now. I can't honey. Think what would happen if I left right now. We have to get some things worked out before I leave or I think the church will fall apart. As a whole our church is spiritually sick and it needs to be well before I leave, well unless they kick me out."

"Why do you think this keeps going on then?"

"I really don't know. Actually, I have two ideas. One is, my time of effective ministry is over here. I might not be relating to the people, or maybe God wants to move me, or I've passed my prime. It's been tough getting up in the pulpit these last three weeks and giving a sermon I've spent so much time on, and it seems to not even make a dent in a single person. They may say 'Great sermon Preach', or 'I really needed to hear that' but I see no evidence of it in their lives. Not everybody, but the majority. I have to question myself here, maybe I have lost my effectiveness. But the thing is, I study and I pray for the Holy Spirit to use me, and that it would be His Words, not mine, and there are times I feel my heart breaking for these people and I know it is God breaking my pride, so then I am reminded of the nation of Israel and Samuel. When they wanted a King and God told Samuel it's not you they are rejecting its me. It hurts so bad when people say 'One man didn't build this church' I know that. More than anyone, you and I have seen God work here, and the only reason I think that is because we were willing to be used, and we never lost sight of where our blessings came from. But if people think that it was us, not just church people but people in the community, then we are taking the focus, unintentionally, off of God and placing it on us. Just like John the Baptist's ministry began declining when Jesus came on the scene and the focus needed to be placed on Him. John realized this. 'He must increase and I must decrease'."

"I've never thought of that before, I always just thought it was Satan attacking and evil men and spiritual warfare and all that. But don't you think it would be an easier transition if God was taking the focus off of us, or wanting us to move or something."

"Well that's my other idea. And it could be a combination of both. See, well, I got a letter about three or four weeks ago, I hadn't shown it to you because I thought it might be a prank, but now I don't know."

"I'm sorry to interrupt sir," the voice startled James, he hadn't even seen the waiter standing there, "But have you decided?"

"Yeah I know what I want. Hannah?"

"Uh, yeah, you go first though."

"I'll have the bacon cheeseburger. No tomatoes or lettuce."

"Alright, and for you ma'am?"

"How about the prime rib medium rare."

"Alright, I'll be out with those in a few minutes."

"Thanks."

"So what was I saying? Oh yeah the letter. Well I'll just let you read it."

James handed the letter to Hannah and watched her expressions as she read the letter. James had learned to read into peoples expressions as much as what they say. Natural expressions or reactions never lied. People could lie with their lips, on paper, and rehearsed they could lie to your face and maybe they even believed it, but reactions never lied. This was a skill he had developed in his many years counseling. Sometimes he felt like an expert interrogator, watching the faces of spies as the CIA tried getting information from them. Right now, he was reading the letter along with her, pacing it in his head and watching her expressions. He had expected to see confusion, or disbelief, but instead it was fear. This puzzled James. If it scared her, she had to believe it and probably had already considered it. Fear usually came in the form of confirming something that had already been conceived in the persons mind. He knew that women really did have some sort of intuition, and his wife was blessed with being able to read people well.

"When did you get this?" Hannah had finished reading and was studying the picture.

"It was a while ago. Like I said, at first I thought it might be a prank but the more I've watched Adam and Candy, the more I believe it."

"I believe it. But why would they do these kind of things?"

"I've been trying to answer that question myself. Maybe they're not saved, or have an axe to grind, maybe one of their dads was a preacher and got the shaft or didn't spend enough time with them, I don't know."

"Do you think they might be possessed?"

"I don't want to go that far. I guess it's possible. Even one of the disciples was Satan, so anything is possible, but I hate to jump to any conclusions. I just don't know what to do now."

"Maybe you should call your dad."

"I guess I could swallow my pride."

"You guys got a lot worked out in California, I thought."

"We did, but this is different."

"How so?"

James really wasn't wanting to discuss this right now, he knew he was wrong, and he knew she knew he was wrong, and he was going to call his dad, but he didn't want to go through a whole ordeal just so he could look stupid.

"It just is!"

Hannah looked hurt. He hadn't meant for it to come out like that. He hadn't snapped at her in years. When they were first married James really had to watch the way he talked to her. He used to answer hatefully and ask questions in a demanding tone, mostly unintentional, they had come out of habit. Both of his parents were short when they spoke, and to someone unaccustomed to this it would sound hateful. This was something he had worked on since they were first married when he saw how it hurt her.

"I'm sorry." James said truly remorseful. "It isn't any different, and I am going to call him. Sorry."

Hannah couldn't help but forgive James. She had always been able to tell when he was sincere and right now, he was. He was probably hurt worse by his rudeness than she was.

"It's alright honey I shouldn't have pushed. You have enough stress as it is, I don't need to add any."

The rest of the meal was spent in conversation about their son's new found love life, how soon Brad and Jenny were going to be parents, and James mentioned they should give some money anonymously to the Nelsons. He knew they had been having a hard time financially and their oldest son was struggling in school and it had been strongly recommended that they put him in a private school. Hannah agreed and they decided to send it off tomorrow. It was strange how good it felt to help someone when they knew that person needed it. James could remember when they were younger and first married they had made decent money, with him working at his dad's church and Hannah writing for the paper, and they had helped people then too. However, they never helped anonymously like they did now.

On the way home, Hannah talked James into stopping by the hospital just to see if the doctor had kept Jenny. James had argued weakly, saying they would have called if he had, but he hoped they were there too. It was almost like they were having their third grandbaby. The ringing of their cell phone interrupted their disagreement on the sex of the baby. James had guaranteed it was a boy, but Hannah 'just knew' it was a girl.

"She's carrying it like a basketball." She had said. "A football's a boy, a basketball's a girl."

It took three rings for her to find the phone and answer it.

"Hello."

"Mom?"

"Yeah."

"Hey where you guys at?"

"We're just pulling in to the parking lot at the hospital."

"Oh, so then you heard."

"What? Did they have a girl?"

"Who?"

"Brad and Jenny, doof, who else."

"No, no nothing like that. Rachael Pattison got in a wreck, and they rushed her to the emergency room. Cass' just got a call from little Gerry, and she said Rachael is hurt pretty bad, I guess they're really scared. You should probably go by, don't you think?"

"Yeah we will. Man, that's scary. You be super careful driving home tonight. I'm serious."

"I will. I'll probably go home in a little while, I think they're all going to go see her in a little bit."

"Good. Thanks for calling Jace. Bye."

"Hasta."

James looked at his wife as she closed the phone and put it in her purse. There was deep concern all across her face.

"What's up?"

"I've got some bad news."

Chapter 9

"You have to call him back."

"I don't really want to talk to him at all. He's probably just calling to complain or lie about something else."

"It doesn't matter. You can't just blow him off forever. This is the third time he's called in two days, and you know you will see him at church. You guys work together for goodness sakes."

"I know but I'm just sick of hearing him complain." Brad said as he picked up the church directory and turned to the N's.

He ran his finger down the column to where the Nelsons should be, before he realized he had picked up the older directory by mistake. He often thumbed through it getting a good laugh at some of the member's older pictures, or one of his high school kids picture's from sixth grade. He wasn't chuckling now however. He shoved the directory back into its temporary home, known as the junk drawer, and retrieved their phone book from the recesses of the drawer. This time when he turned to the N's and followed it down to Nelson he found the two Marks and chose the one on Shadow Mountain Lane. Mark and Sara had moved to Lendel three years ago from the Dallas area. Mark had taken the job as Music Minister and had also taught the college and career class. About six months ago Sara started working at the church as the secretary, it was a token job from the church since they had volunteers to do it but they needed the money to help make ends meet. Apparently, they incurred a lot of debt from their move and they had bought a really nice house up in the Shadow Mountain area, which, Mark regretfully admitted, had over loaded their budget. They had sold their house in Texas and thought they would have enough to pay off their house here but had blown it on a car, boat, etc. He really seemed to hold a grudge against James ever since James had sent him to counseling for debt. He had put Mark on a type of probation until he could get his payments current, and manageable, and had made Mark apologize to the church. Even after James hired Sara, only to help them out, Mark still held a grudge.

Brad began dialing their number hoping for their answering machine to pick up, even though he thought they had the most annoying message. Mark had changed the words to Coming Again to 'Call me Again' and sang an entire spoof of the old hymn. At least it was only one verse and the chorus, he could have rewritten all three verses if he had wanted to be really annoying. Brad wasn't that lucky however, after the second ring Silas picked up.

"Nelson's residence. Silas speaking."

"Hey Silas, is your dad there?"

"May I ask who's calling?"

"Henry Kissinger"

"Hold on just a minute."

Brad could hear Silas set the phone down and then he heard Marks voice

"Who?" he couldn't hear the response but in just a couple seconds he heard Mark fumbling with the phone.

"Hello."

"Hi Mark its Brad. I'm just returning your call."

"Oh hi Brad. I just called to let you know I am going to resign this Sunday."

"You are? Seriously?"

"Yeah."

"Why?"

"Well, you know that meeting we had the day after camp?"

"How could I forget?"

"Well it really opened my eyes. This is a sinking ship Brad. Didn't you hear what was going on at that meeting. I don't want to be working for a man who is taking money from people, who can't admit when he is wrong, who takes advantage of everyone around him, who doesn't practice what he preaches. I mean he makes me stand up and apologize to the whole church for getting in debt, and what does he do, he just steals to make up for it."

Brad was silent. He was too mad right now to say anything, he was afraid of what might come out.

"I can't work for him anymore. He lies to me all the time, he's demanding and unreasonable." Mark added.

Brad finally said something. "So have you told the Pastor yet?"

"No way, you're the first person I've told. Well Adam knows, in fact that's where I'm going to work. He offered me a job about a month ago as a real estate agent. I can do that and still teach the college class if I decide to stay at this church. Anyway, Adam and I thought it might be better to tell him at a deacons meeting or somewhere there's other people since you never know how he will react. Know what I mean?"

"No. I don't know what you mean at all. You're basically being a jerk. So, when you dedicated your life to full time service was it just a joke to you? Do you think God called you here or was this just a job?"

"Listen Brad. We got duped into this. We were led to believe the salary was more, the cost of living less, I would ONLY be doing music, and James was a lot different the first couple times we met. I didn't sign up for this and neither did you. Can't you see the signs all around. If this was God's will, wouldn't it be a lot easier? Wouldn't things just fall in line? Wake up Brad."

"Do you remember when Jesus said 'Oh wicked generation that seeketh after a sign'. And where do you get the idea that being in God's will means it is going to be easy? Do you have any Scripture to back that up?" Brad was starting to get on a roll. "Don't you remember Joseph? He was a slave for Potipher, kidnaped, wrongfully imprisoned, and yet he was in Gods will. What about Paul? How many times was he thrown in jail for preaching the gospel? Or Hosea? God commanded him to marry an unfaithful prostitute to teach a living example of His forgiveness and love. Do you think that was easy? Or Jesus himself? He had to die on a cross and even prayed "If this cup could pass from me, but not my will, yours." Do you think it was easy for him? What would you do if you were actually being persecuted? Are you going to pack your bags and run every time you have a problem? And you know how I feel about the way you are lying about James. I know you're lying and you know you're lying. I don't even know why you tried to make me think he was a bad Pastor. That's idiotic. I can honestly say I am more disappointed with you than I ever thought I could be. To be honest I am glad you're resigning. I think its wrong for you, but good for the church. You're a cancer to the leadership of this church."

"Leadership?!!! What leadership? The only people acting like leaders are the deacons. You have to lead someone to be a leader. You and James and the like aren't leaders you're manipulators--"

"--Hold on a minute Mark, this is getting ridiculous. We better quit before one of us says something we regret. This is getting us no where. I know how you feel and you know how I do. Let's just leave it at that. Alright?"

"Whatever."

"Fine. Bye."

"Yeah."

Brad hung up the phone softly and shook his head, smiling. This reaction surprised even him. He had been so angry just moments before, but now felt a sense of relief. He had been able to keep his cool and make his point clearly, and scripturally based. It felt like such a load was lifted from his shoulders and his mind now that he finally got to share his opinion with someone other than poor Jenny. It probably didn't really make any effect on Mark, but if it just made him think about it, that was a start. Brad believed if someone thought about the situation and weighed the evidence there was no way they would believe the lies being spread about his pastor.

Jenny looked up from the baby book she was reading when Brad walked into the room. Their ceiling fan light, right above her head, really brought out the red in her hair. She was officially a 'strawberry blonde' but ever since she got pregnant, her hair had turned dark red. Her mother, who had scarlet red hair, had been blonde, but with each child's birth a little more red overtook the golden strands. Brad often pictured their baby coming out with a full head of Jenny's red and his curly hair.

"What did Mark want?" She asked laying her book on her chest and taking off her glasses.

Brad shook his head and chewed his bottom lip. "I guess he's going to resign. What a wimp. He couldn't stand up for the pastor and now he is completely bailing out."

"Seriously, he's quitting?"

"Yeah. And he's trying to make it sound like it's the Pastor's fault."

"When is he quitting?"

"Sunday, I guess."

"Does James know?"

"No, and he's not going to tell him either. I guess he's just going to go around telling everyone else first. He's such a jerk."

"Are you going to tell James?" Jenny asked.

"Yeah, don't you think I should?"

Jenny nodded in agreement.

"In fact I think I'll call him right now."

Brad picked up the cordless phone sitting behind the couch and dialed James' number. The voice mail picked up and Brad left a message, asking James to call him as soon as possible.

* * * *

James and Hannah rushed toward the Emergency waiting room not even bothering to ask the receptionist where the Pattison's were. James knew his way around the hospital as good as about anybody, with all the visits he had made for births, deaths, illnesses, and accidents. This was however, one of the most nervous trips he had made down the ER hallway. As soon as they entered the waiting room, they saw Jerry holding Pam rubbing her back softly and whispering to her. James walked up behind them and put a hand on Jerry's shoulder.

"How is she?"

"I don't know James. The doctor hasn't told us anything yet. We haven't seen anyone."

Just then, a short man wearing a white lab coat came into the room. "Mr. and Mrs. Pattison?" He was looking towards Jerry and James waiting for one of them to volunteer as Mr. Pattison. Jerry stepped forward, with his arm around Pam.

"Yes?"

The short man turned toward James and Hannah, "Could you excuse us for a minute?" James and Hannah nodded their heads and walked out the door, patting Jerry on the back on their way out.

They headed to the coffee machine at the end of the hall and Hannah finally asked, "Do you think its bad?"

"I don't know. Probably. I feel bad for Jerry. His heart must be pounding."

Just then, he heard Jerry's voice get very loud.

"That's impossible!!!"

There was a moment of silence and then Jerry threw the doors open and headed down the hall not even stopping to talk to James and Hannah. They looked at each other, the worry written all over their faces. They hurried in the waiting room to see Pam.

"Are you okay?" Hannah asked.

"Yeah, I guess. The good news is Rachael's okay. She should be moved into her own room in about an hour and we can see her then. She'll probably get to go home tomorrow."

"That's fantastic!" James exclaimed.

"Yeah, except that, well, they found a trace of alcohol in her blood stream. Apparently, she had been drinking right before she got in the accident. The doctor said they will have to put it in their report. Jerry completely freaked out. He kept saying 'but she doesn't drink, she doesn't drink'. I hope he's alright, he just took off and I don't know where he's going."

"I'm so sorry Pam." Hannah said giving her a hug.

She really didn't know what to say. She couldn't even begin to comprehend all the different emotions Pam had gone through in the last few hours.

Hannah was really concerned about Jerry, she couldn't imagine him acting the way he had, Rachael always seemed to be the apple of his eye, and to not even wait around to see her, she just couldn't believe it. Just then, Jerry came through the door with his head down. He came back and sat down on a bench just outside the waiting room. James walked over and sat beside him, putting his long arm around Jerry's shoulders and his big hand squeezing his arm. Hannah could see them talking and Jerry shaking his head. She could see him start to break down and she could tell by his sobbing shoulders the tears were falling.

* * * *

"Maybe you should try him again."

Jenny's voice made Brad jump, spilling paint on the carpet in the baby's room.

He looked up at her and shook his head.

"Sorry." She said.

"That's okay I'll just put the dresser over it and nobody will know. That's what I did with the toy box." He was just joking but Jenny wasn't sure. "What did you want?"

"I thought maybe you should try calling him again."

"Who?"

"Pastor Knoll. Maybe he didn't get the message and he needs to know."

"Okay, I'll call him in just a second, I got to clean up this paint real quick."

Brad headed to the kitchen, got a towel, and spent the next ten minutes scrubbing the floor as best he could. The stain still didn't come out like what he wanted but it would have to do.

Picking up the phone he hit the redial button and 15 seconds later he was on the phone with Jason.

"Hospital? Why?"

"You didn't hear? Rachael got in an accident and she's hurt pretty bad, so they stayed there with the Pattisons."

"Seriously, Rachael got in a wreck? Is she okay?"

"I don't know, I haven't heard anything. I'm worried though. I thought they would have called by now."

"Alright Jace, thanks. Hey, if your parents happen to call, tell them we're headed there. Thanks."

"Alright. Bye."

Brad hung up the phone, butterfly's beginning to fill his stomach. *I should have called Jerry and Pam, or at least stopped her from driving. I knew she shouldn't have been driving.*

"Wow, that was quick. Was he not there?"

"No."

Brad was looking through Jenny to Jerry and Pam in the emergency room. He couldn't imagine what they must be feeling. He had never really understood the love a parent had for their child until Jenny had gotten pregnant. He hadn't even seen or met their soon to be child, yet he loved it so much, and constantly worried for the baby's safety.

"Hellllllooo." Jenny was waving her hand in front of his face.

"Sorry honey. Rachael got in a wreck and she's in the hospital. I guess she's in pretty bad shape. I told Jason we were headed there. Are you gonna be okay if we go?"

* * * *

Jerry's head hung low even as the doctor delivered the good news.

"We moved her to her own room. She should be coming to anytime now so you guys are free to stay in there if you would like. We're just going to monitor her for the night and if nothing shows up she'll be free to go in the morning."

Jerry was relieved that his daughter was going to be okay, but he was still feeling very disconcerted. He was ashamed of the way he had acted, he felt bad for the unfounded comments he had made about Jason when his own daughter had been drinking and driving. He was at war inside with his feelings toward James, what to do about Rachael, and what to do about himself. Part of him longed for things to be the way they used to be, the way they were six months ago, but part of him realized it would never be that way again. He decided he would ask James if they could keep this between themselves at least until he figured out what to do about Rachael. *No one needs to know. It will only damage her reputation, and mine too. I'm sure James will understand.*

"Thank you doctor." Pam's voice yanked Jerry back to the hospital waiting room where he realized the doctor had finished explaining Rachael's injuries.

He had heard mumbling and then 'she needs her rest' more mumbling, 'very lucky girl' more mumbling, and finally Pam's voice. Jerry tried to make it look like he had been listening.

"Yes doctor, thanks for all your help. We owe you so much. We will make sure Rachael gets all the rest she needs. Thanks again."

As soon as the doctor left, Jerry began frantically looking around for James. He had seen him here a few minutes ago but was now nowhere to be seen.

"What's the matter?" Pam could see the urgency in Jerry's face.

"Do you know where James is?"

"Yeah, they went down to the cafeteria. They said they'd be back in a few minutes."

Jerry headed to the elevator without even saying a word to Pam. No 'bye', no 'be right back', not even a 'thanks', just straight to the elevator. He hit the L button on the control panel and felt the floor dropping below him. Usually he jumped when he headed down, something he had done since he was a boy and it had just stuck with him. He always tried to hit his head on the roof. He even did it sometimes when other people were in there with him. This time however, he was too distressed to even think about it. For some reason he could just picture James on the phone with everyone he knew telling them how 'Jerry's daughter got in a drunk driving accident.' He could see him trying to smear his name to everyone in the church, especially the other deacons who respected him so much.

As the elevator door began to open, the flag of hope that had slowly begun to raise was ripped from the pole and shredded with the rage that inundated Jerry's mind and elevated itself to full mast on the flag pole. Right in the foyer of the hospital, James and Hannah were shaking hands with Brad and Jenny. *He couldn't even wait five minutes could he. I wonder how many people he called besides Brad.* The rage that Jerry felt now however was flamed into white anger when he got close enough to hear what was being said.

"I almost feel like it's my fault."

"Don't worry about that. There's nothing you could have done."

"I know but I just keep thinking, maybe I could have stopped her. She looked really scared when she saw us."

Here Jerry boiled over. His protective shield of insecurities melted away under the heat of his anger.

"You were spying on my daughter!"

"What? Jerry? No. I just happened to see her."

"So you spied on my daughter and then didn't even have the decency to tell me. She could have died. What kind of youth pastor are you?"

"Jerry wait a minute. Calm down for a second." James voice was calm and soothing.

He had been in potentially violent situations before and he saw all the warning signs with this one. He moved toward Jerry and placed his hand on Jerry's shoulder. Jerry shrugged it off, staring angrily at Brad. Brad was about 2 inches shorter than Jerry's 5'11'' and maybe 30 lbs lighter. This was all giving Jerry confidence, and he started moving toward Brad disregarding all comfort zones. Finally, James cut him off stepping between Brad and Jerry. James towered over both of them and he still was in pretty good shape. He had been quite an athlete in high school, lettering in three sports, and he continued to spend time at the gym to be able to compete with Jason. He wasn't going to fight Jerry, but Jerry didn't know this and as excited as he was to jump all over Brad he was that worried about tangling with Pastor Knoll. He backed off a couple steps still glaring at Brad. Brad was speechless. He was standing there looking wide-eyed at Jerry like a deer caught in the headlights. Jerry was glaring around Pastor Knoll, his fists clinching and releasing. His breath was heavy and he was shaking so hard it had a hint of vibrato.

"Let's go for a walk Jerry." James stepped towards him talking to him as he would to his son.

Everyone in the lobby had turned their attention to this group. Most of them recognizing James or Brad, and a lot knowing Jerry for years. It was an embarrassing situation that James wanted to end but Jerry didn't want to cooperate.

"I can't believe you didn't tell me."

"I-I-I'm sorry Jerry. I didn't…well I… I… I'm sorry."

James tugged on Jerry's arm and they turned to walk outside. Just then, the voices came back. Jerry jerked his arm away from James and spun around facing Brad again.

"What did you say?"

"Nothing."

"Don't lie to me. I heard you laughing."

"I didn't Jerry. Why would I?"

"Because you think you fooled me, but I know."

"I don't even know what you're talking about." Brad was starting to get angry now too.

This was what James was worried about. He could handle it if just one of them was angry, but it was a lot tougher with both. He motioned to Hannah to get Brad out of there but she didn't understand his extremely primitive sign language. He was too busy trying to communicate to her he didn't see the two men moving up beside them.

"Is there a problem here gentlemen?"

All heads turned toward the voice. Two officers were standing off-set from one another, clad in their common blue uniforms, both having their right hands resting on their night sticks. No one had a verbal response. Brad's face began filling with color as he turned his head. Jerry's eyes showed his surprise to see the police officers standing there, and maybe a realization of how disruptive he had been was setting in as he lowered his head pushing through the small crowd and silently headed to the exit.

"No sir, I think its pretty much taken care of." James finally spoke ending the uncomfortable silence that had fallen over the entire lobby.

The older officer seemed to be satisfied with the dissemination of the small stand off, but the other faded back and began to follow behind Jerry. "Alright then, you guys might want to clear out of here, and remember to keep it down." He was kind of smiling as he said this.

"Thank you officer, we will." James turned to walk away and he saw Hannah talking with Pam and Jenny but Brad was no where to be seen.

Jerry was unlocking his car, mumbling angrily, when he saw Brad coming out of the front door, heading across the parking lot apparently toward his car. He put the keys back in his pocket and began his crouch-over run, darting behind the cars in the parking lot, making his way, undetected, toward Brad. What Jerry didn't know is he was also being followed. The young police officer that, more out of curiosity than anything else, had followed him outside, was now earnestly trailing Jerry not letting him get too far away. Jerry was now two cars away from Brad. He could hear Brad's hard footsteps, and then they stopped. He heard him fumbling with his keys and decided to strike now.

"Hey!" Jerry yelled scaring Brad to death.

Brad jumped and whirled around. Jerry was two feet away from him and he closed the gap in one step. He shoved Brad up against his car. Brad was staring him down this time pushing his hands away from his chest, trying to straighten up. Jerry had come up on Brad so quick and so close he was having to lean back over the roof of his car.

"Don't you ever laugh at me again!"

"I didn't laugh at you Jerry."

Jerry brought his left hand up quickly and grabbed Brad by the throat, cocking his right arm back, his fist waiting for the signal from his brain to smash into Brad's face. But for some reason the signal delayed. Only for a couple seconds. Brad was anticipating the crunch of knuckles against his mouth, but he didn't feel it. The four second delay was all Officer Neil needed. He had begun racing toward them as soon as Jerry shoved him against the car, and made a diving tackle to peel him off Brad. They rolled on the ground and Neil hopped to his
feet first. Jerry wouldn't get up off the ground he just laid there, thoroughly ashamed.

"Get up!" Neil commanded him. Jerry looked up and slowly stood to his feet.

Neil turned toward Brad. "I saw the whole thing. You can press charges if you would like and I'll take him to the station right now."

"PRESS CHARGES! For what?!!!!"

"For harassment. Now keep your mouth shut."

"No. I don't want to press charges. He's just upset about his daughter. Thanks though officer." Brad answered.

"Alright, its up to you. I am going to wait here until one of you leaves though."

"I was just coming out to my car to get my wallet. I was gonna get a cup of coffee and realized I had left it out here." Brad said.

"Then I guess you're going to have to go." Neil pointed in the direction of Jerry's car.

Jerry turned, angrily walking back to his car. They could both hear him mumbling the entire way. About halfway to his car he spun around, and with a look of triumph shouted at Brad.

"I'll see you Sunday, you'll get yours then."

Brad shook his head.

"Are you sure you don't want to press charges?"

"Yeah, I'm sure. We're having a business meeting at church Sunday and I imagine that's what he's talking about."

"At church? You guys go to church together? No wonder I've never gone. What church is it?"

Brad felt like he had just been slapped in the face. What a testimony. What a living example. What a 'little Christ' he had been. So, this is what this guy would think of when he heard Lendel Community Church. This is what he would think of anytime anyone tried to share the gospel to him. *Love one another and the world will know you are mine.* Jesus had said this to his disciples and Brad had made a mockery of it. The tears began to fill his eyes, lowering his head he whispered:

"Lendel Community."

"Lendel Community? Oh my gosh. That big church over by Skyline Drive? The one with the College? Oh man, just wait till I tell my wife about this. We've driven by there and she always wants to go. She keeps saying, 'something good must be going on over there'. Thanks buddy. You guys saved me my Sunday morning football games." With a slap on Brad's back Officer Neil headed back to the hospital. He stopped and tipped his hat to James who had been walking up while the men were talking.

He saw the tears streaming down Brad's face.

"I really screwed up."

Pastor James put his arm around Brad and both men knelt right there in the parking lot and prayed. The tears streaming down Brad's cheeks hit the pavement and ran away, releasing sorrows of the past two months.

Chapter 10

The yellow slashes in the road were being melted into one long line. James shook his head to wake himself up a bit. He always got up around 5 a.m. but this morning it seemed to come a lot sooner. He had been tired when he climbed into his car, and the rising sun, as he topped the second range of mountains, had made it all the harder to stay awake. He had stopped in Frisco to get a cup of coffee, to help keep him awake the rest of the way. His legs ached and the coffee burned his stomach. He thought about grabbing a snack cake or something but his queasy stomach changed his mind. They had donuts waiting when he got to the Fellowship meeting, but he passed on those also.

The meeting was exceptionally good, the speaker was a former Pastor in Tampa, who was starting a home missions ministry called "Koinonia," a Greek word for fellowship. The focus of his ministry was not on the local church, however, but the Pastors of these churches. He shared the testimonies of several Pastors who had faced difficulty, feelings of rejection, insecurities, doubts of their ability to lead, and numerous other problems. Their ministry was to help these men regain their confidence in God and His ability to lead their lives, as well as in some cases, find them a new place to serve if their reputation or ability to effectively share the gospel had been damaged in a particular geographical area. James had stayed around after the meeting to talk to some of his preacher friends and for the first time in a while really felt good, felt close to someone other than his wife, felt like he had friends that could encourage him, or counsel him. He didn't want to leave. Finally, around 4:00 he left.

Now, he was paying for not having eaten all day, not getting enough sleep lately, and being one of the last ones to leave the meeting. He kept shaking his head every time the slashes started to blur together. All he could think about right now was his bed. His soft pillow, the cool breeze blowing through his window. In a strange way, dreaming about sleep was keeping him awake. *Just ten more miles.* He looked at his speedometer and he had the cruise set at 65. He tried figuring out exactly how long it would take him. He did this every time he drove somewhere and usually it was pretty easy. Right now however, his sleep deprived mind was having trouble dividing the simplest of equations. He gave up after his mind gave him the total of twenty-five minutes. Nine minutes twenty-three seconds later, he pulled into his drive. Completely exhausted he walked through the kitchen door, giving his wife a kiss, he headed for the bathroom to start his bath water.

"Hey, honey. Aren't you going to eat first?" Hannah yelled from the kitchen.

"Yeah, as soon as I'm done with my bath. I just want to get in, relax, eat something, then go to bed." James voice was somewhat muffled by the sound of the water.

"Um, okay, but Bill called and said they need to have an emergency meeting tonight. He wanted you to call him as soon as you got in."

"You have got to be kidding me. Another meeting. I am so tired of meetings. It would be one thing if we got something accomplished, but we never do. Sometimes they decide they want to support me, but then something happens and they change their mind, sometimes they get angry, sometimes our discussions are good, but nothing ever comes out of them. What we need to do is bring it before the church, but none of the deacons want to do that until they can say we are united on a decision. I am just so tired of having meetings."

"I'm sorry honey. I wish there was something I could do."

"No, that's okay. Did Bill say if he was going to be at home or at work?"

"I think he said at home."

"I guess I better call then." James emerged from the bathroom with a towel tied around his waist. He picked up the phone, grabbed the phone book, found the number and dialed.

"Hello."

"Bill?"

"This is him."

"Yeah hi, this is James."

"Oh hi James. I called a little bit ago but your wife said you were in Denver."

"Yeah I went to a Fellowship meeting."

"Oh. Well I just called to inform you that we need to have a meeting tonight. It's pretty important. I just got off the phone with some people and they gave me some pretty disturbing news I think we need to discuss."

"Like what?" Strangely, James wasn't too concerned. Bill always had a way of making everything so melodramatic.

"Well, like the second page of the paper this morning. And also why three people are resigning after yesterday."

"What, after Sunday, what are you talking about? Who are you talking about?"

"I'll just tell you about it tonight. I already called everyone and they're going to the church at about seven. It will probably go pretty late."

"Well I guess I'll be there then. Bye."

"Bye."

Hannah could tell by her husbands face the call had not been so good. She wanted to ask him, but decided to let him tell her if he wanted to. She felt so sorry for him. She didn't understand why all this was happening, but she trusted God that it was for the best. He didn't deserve the way he was treated, he had given his life to these people, to the community, and they had trampled on it. They had used it, drank every bit of the love and joy out it, and then crushed it under their foot like a pop can. She really was having a difficult time loving the people, the town, even the ministry. It was her deep faith in God that kept her sane, and gave her hope.

"Did we get a paper today?" James voice sounded rough and

broken. There was even a hint of defeat she had never heard in his voice before.

“Yes. I put it on the table. I haven’t even had a chance to look at it yet.”

James unrolled it, and turned to the second page. His eyes focused quickly on the picture and caption Bill was obviously talking about. He shook his head, closed the paper, placing it neatly back on the table, and headed for his bath. Hannah picked up the paper and turned to the second page. On the top right hand corner was a picture of James and Brad talking to the police officers. Brad had his head down and James looked as if he was explaining his case to the arresting officers. The picture was large covering one-fourth of the page. The caption underneath read: “Pastor James Knoll of Lendel Community Church trying to explain to Officers Keith Richards and Neil Lyons, why he and Youth Pastor Brad Howe, had created such a violent disturbance, that the Lendel Hospital Security had to be called.” Seeing this, she was even more amazed at her husband. He hadn’t shouted, he hadn’t said ‘this isn’t fair’, he just shook his head and walked away. She knew this was probably what their meeting was going to be about tonight. She decided she would call Jenny and Nancy and see if they would come over and pray with her during the meeting.

James got ready and left without saying a word. He did however give her a kiss on the lips before heading out to war. She hurried to the phone as soon as he left and called Jenny first. She agreed to come over, and complained quite a bit about the picture in the paper. She seemed to be very frustrated, and Hannah couldn’t blame her. She was nine plus months pregnant, and that alone would make someone irritated, but couple that with everything else that was going on, and anyone would be angry. Hannah finally got her off the phone promising they would continue to talk about it when she got there. Next, she called Nancy. At first Nancy seemed very confused, until they realized that Bob had not been told of the meeting. Nancy seemed very excited and Bob decided he would go to the meeting even without an invitation.

It wasn’t long until Hannah heard the door bell ring and she saw Nancy standing out front. Hannah opened the door, and Nancy turned to wave. Apparently, Bob had dropped her off and was headed to the church. He looked kind of funny smashed into their tiny hatch back. She couldn't imagine how all 260 pounds of him had squeezed in there. They had looked at the exact same car but James couldn't fit in it and he was 2 inches shorter and 50 lbs. lighter than Bob.

"Where's your truck?" She asked. Bob always drove the truck.

"Oh, he was changing the spark plugs, and wires and a bunch of other stuff when you called, so he just left it to head to the meeting."

"Wow. He didn't have to do that."

"Yes, he did. He loves your husband, and he loves this church. You don't know how much James has helped our family. We might not be together right now if it wasn't for him. Not only our family, he has helped so many. Just look around the church. The families that are here aren't people dissatisfied with their old church, most of them are first generation Christians. People who got saved and joined our church since James has come. It still amazes me every time I see the Hopps in church. And you don't know what it was like seeing Kale sing last week. If you had grown up here, you'd know. It's unbelievable what God has done through you guys. Unbelievable."

* * * *

James looked up from the blank sheet of paper in front of him when he heard someone coming downstairs. It was Bob.

"Sorry I'm late. My phone must not be working because I only found out about this a little while ago." Bob's sarcasm was easy to see.

James noted how the mood seemed to change with just the addition of Bob. He couldn't decide if it was his size, or his ghetto wisdom, but there was something about him that intimidated these men. Even Adam. James had seen him inadvertently twitch when Bob walked through the door. Even now, he could see Adam's jaw bone moving in and out, as he clinched his teeth. Bob strolled right over to the table and pulled out a chair sitting next to Steve. Before the appearance of Bob, the deacons had been hammering away at James. They had put him on trial and not let anyone speak out for him. Brad couldn't, they had already torn apart any credibility he may have had.

Steve hadn't said a word, and he wouldn't even make eye contact with James. Phillip tried to defend, but every time he opened his mouth, they cut him off before he had a chance to say much. He had been sitting back, slumped low in his chair, arms crossed, until the emergence of Bob. He had quickly perked up, now sitting on the edge of his chair leaning on the table. Bill who had been talking for the last 15 minutes seemed totally flustered. Phillip wouldn't let him off however.

"You were saying Bill?"

"Um, well, I guess I was finished."

"No you weren't. You stopped in mid sentence about how Pastor wasn't fooling anyone anymore. How the majority of the church either wanted him to resign or change."

"The majority of the church?" Bob didn't take long to jump in. "What do you mean by majority?"

"Well the larger percentage."

"I think you are probably wrong about that. I would say the majority of our church is in support of the Pastor. Maybe your little clique complains too much and gets each other riled up over things, and maybe you are talking about the same two or three people, and maybe you aren't even talking about anyone, and maybe we should take it to the church and let them decide." Bob argued.

"We can't take it to the church when we aren't even in agreement on what to do. We've already lost too many families, that no one seems to care about, and in something like this we might lose more."

"After the body eats and gets full, there's always waste. It has to go somewhere."

"See, that's exactly the attitude I'm talking about. That's James attitude and it seems now you have picked it up as well." Jerry finally said something after being silent for the entirety of the meeting so far.

"No, it's just that you can't compromise your beliefs for everyone that decides to leave. You cannot cater to everyone's whim or feeling of guilt. You have to remain true to the only absolute truth and that is the Word of God." Pastor Knoll had made this point to the men on several occasions and hoped they would remember this time.

"Do you even know why some of these people left?" Jerry was gaining more confidence with every question.

He liked the attention of everyone listening to him when he talked, all eyes turned toward him, he lived for this now. This and the checks from his investment with Adam. He had received his first one the same day as Rachael's wreck after he left the hospital. He had gone straight home after the altercation with Brad and had turned on ESPN. He was flipping through the mail and found his check from Adam. He opened it and it was for $7500.00. He couldn't believe it, he had talked to Adam earlier in the week and Adam told him this would probably be the smallest check he would ever get. This first month the tenancy wasn't quite full and they had to pay for licensing and had replaced a lot of appliances. He said it was probably only going to be about 80% of the regular amount until they got their rentals to full capacity. Adam called him that evening to express his sorrow for what happened to Rachael, and also told him they had filled the last apartment that day. He could expect maybe double the next month. *How God blesses even in times of trial when you are faithful to him.* Jerry just knew that's what this was. A blessing.

"Yes I do know why almost everyone has left. I don't, however, know why Mark is resigning." Pastor Knoll also knew there were reasons he couldn't share with the men to protect some people from undo shame. This he would never share with these men, or anyone.

"Well I think I can speak for Mark. He didn't even show tonight because he was afraid of your reaction. He said you are the most demanding, untruthful boss he has ever had. You really owe him an apology."

"An apology? I don't even know what I have done."

"Then you need to go to him and find out."

"I will. Tonight when I leave."

The meeting continued not really deciding anything as usual. The topic of the picture came up but Adam and Jerry silenced it pretty quickly. Phillip did, however, resign as deacon, and Steve resigned and said he wanted to move his membership. James tried talking

Phillip out of resigning but he wouldn't do it. He said he would remain a member and try to fight that way but no longer thought he could be a deacon.

Jerry and Adam left together talking and laughing. Brad slipped out not saying a word. Bill and Jack talked quietly. Steve and Phillip hugged James and left. Bob waited and walked James to his car. They talked and James said he'd meet him for breakfast in the morning. After they drove away, James headed up Skyline Drive. He stopped at his familiar spot. He could see his breath in the car's head lights as he walked in the path to look out over the city. The tears would have come if there had been any more to cry. He looked out over the town of Lendel, his love for the people showed in his dry tears. He wept.

Chapter 11

Jerry was all smiles as he headed into the gymnasium. Volleyball season had started and Gerry was a big surprise making Varsity as a freshman. She was only the second V-ball player in the history of the Lendel Chargers to be on Varsity as a freshman. Jerry and Pam took their seats in the third row, right above the girl's bench. He saw Rachael trotting onto the court in her cheerleader uniform, her stitches nearly healed. It was amazing to think, only a month ago she was in a hospital bed and they were worried about her making it, and here she was doing back-flips and cart wheels not even missing a beat. Jerry scanned the crowd to see if Adam and Candy had made it yet, when his eyes passed over Brad talking with the Principal of the High School. *I wonder what they could be talking about.*

Frank Gibson had been the principal at Lendel for 10 years. During his ten years, he had never asked James to pray at the graduation. When he finally did, James turned him down. At the time, Jerry agreed with him, praising him for his courage and high standards, but now Jerry realized he should have seen that as the beginning of his ego, of him seeing himself as the only one on the right track. The 'you better do as I say or you aren't going to heaven' attitude. So what, if Frank wanted him to not make any reference to Jesus, or salvation, or redemption, he could still say God. How arrogant James was and nobody even saw it then.

He continued sweeping his eyes around the gymnasium until he finally saw Adam and Candy emerge in the doorway. They were a sharp looking couple, and Jerry found himself wishing he and Pam were a little more hip. He had even gone shopping at the factory outlets and had bought himself a pair of wide-legged carpenters jeans and a Quicksilver shirt. He hadn't worn them yet because Pam had laughed so hard when he put them on that she literally fell on the floor, doubled up, holding her stomach. He would just wait until she was out of town. He waved at them and sat down smugly, thinking he had the coolest friends in the gym.

"Oh man, why did you have to wave. Now they're going to come sit by us." Pam's voice sounded very discouraged.

"Yeah, so. I like Adam, and you'd like Candy too if you would just get to know her a little bit."

"It only takes five minutes. She's the most shallow, materialistic woman I have ever met."

"Sometimes I think you're jealous."

"Should I be?" Pam asked angrily.

"No." Jerry replied. But it was a lie. He had, more than once, imagined himself in Adam's place. In fact, he found himself drawn to those thoughts more and more lately.

"Where are the kids?" Jerry asked, before they had a chance to sit.

"Oh we found a babysitter. Tonight's our night." Adam said, pulling Candy close and giving her a kiss on the top of her head.

Was that a grimace? Jerry asked himself. Lately he had been picking up on a negative attitude, from Candy toward Adam. Or at least he thought he had.

"Thanks for saving us a seat."

"No problem. We always get here early to watch the girls warm up."

They made some small talk and watched Lendel take the first set 15-5. Gerry had actually gotten some time on the court. She had been inserted to set, and pulled when it came time for her to serve. After several exhaustive and boring talks about business and the girls, Adam had finally buttered up Jerry enough to deliver his lethal injection. He let Candy, however, be the prick of the needle.

"Did Adam tell you what we've been talking about?" she asked leaning across Adam to speak directly into Jerry's face. Her eyes locked on his.

"N-no." Jerry felt like a teenager.

He knew nothing would ever happen between him and Candy, but his imagination still made him hope. He felt shy and awkward when she talked to him, and he hoped it wasn't too obvious to his wife or Adam.

"Well we've been thinking about the decline in attendance, and the continuance of a pompous attitude from the pulpit, and we think it might be time to take matters into our own hands."

"What do you mean?"

"Well we've talked to a lot of the people who have left and the majority of them said they tried to work out their problems with James, but he just wouldn't listen. We've talked to some of the people who are still here and they are very dissatisfied with James also--"

Adam broke in. "--we think it's time that the deacon board give him an ultimatum. He must apologize to everyone individually and to the church. He must relinquish his role as the leader of the church to the deacon board and speaker, since his track record proves he is not capable of making a decision that's not out of a selfish desire; and he must stay out of the institute's business, or we will ask him to resign."

Jerry froze. With all the big talk he had been doing, and all the things he had said about his pastor, he didn't want him to leave, he didn't think.

"Won't we lose a whole lot more people if we do that." Jerry's hesitation was obvious to Adam who knew the battle that was raging in Jerry's life right now and he knew the gravity of the next few minutes.

This was it, this was the turning point, this was the battle of Bull-Run, this was the beach at Normandy, this was Pearl Harbor. He had reached a point of decision, and there was no going back now. Once he chose his Captain, troops would be called in and they would begin digging their trenches, building their barracks, and making sure they up-linked their communication systems with their home base. This was the battle.

"Yes, initially. However, in the long run, it would be what is best for this church. James did a lot of good, but he no longer is looking to God for his guidance. I think he got too enamored with himself and started believing HE built this church, and this is HIS church. God can't use him. He's cut himself off from the Master."

"Have you talked to any of the other deacons?"

"Well I thought I'd run it by you first, since you are the speaker." Adam lied.

"Can I have some time to think about it?"

"Sure, sure, like I said, it's just what I've been thinking since I talked to all those people who were dissatisfied."

Jerry was staring off into space. Completely engrossed in the war within, he missed Gerry finally getting to serve and acing for the victory. The jumping and screaming brought him back and he jumped to his feet with everybody else. But the battle wasn't over. Fifteen years had created quite a lot of troops.

* * * *

"Great game Gerry." Brad usually had a fifth quarter after football games, but this weekend, since they had their first volleyball player in the Youth since Brad had been there, they had it after the volleyball game.

"Thanks."

Brad noted Gerry didn't seem as happy as usual. He thought she'd be elated after the game she had. Maybe it was because Rachael hadn't been back to anything involving the Youth since her accident. Not Sunday School, not Youth Night, not fifth quarter, not even an activity. Cassie and Jason had invited her several times, and Jackson, who always had a crush on her, invited her to fifth quarter last week. Last week, what a game he had played. He passed for four touchdowns and over 300 yards at half. Needless to say, he didn't play in the second half. He was a junior and already getting recruited heavily by several division one schools and every small college in the region. He was leaning toward CU but his parents wanted him to go to CSU. It didn't matter, he would be a star wherever he went. He packed on 25 pounds of muscle over the summer and any coach that questioned his size last year, their questions were answered this year.

He was 6'3' and 220 lbs. of speed and muscle.

Brad looked around and counted about 40 kids. They were all regulars, which relieved Brad because of what he needed to talk about tonight. They played the normal capture the flag, and then came in and ate the hot dogs left over from last week. Every one was pretty calm tonight. There wasn't the usual electricity that was in the air at these activities. It didn't take Brad long to get every one calmed down for the lesson. He was nervous for the first time since his first Sunday teaching. He could feel his lips drying out by the second, and he had to take a couple deep breaths.

"Alright everybody, listen up. We are going to do things a little different here tonight than usual. We are going to have a type of open forum." Here Brad paused. He put his hands together, like the praying hands statue, and bounced them softly off his lips. Taking another deep breath he began. "As most of you know, there is a lot of stuff going on at our church. Most of you probably know this, but don't know exactly what it is. Tonight is your opportunity to find out. You can ask whatever, and I'll try to answer it for you."

A hand popped up. "Did Pastor Knoll really steal money?"

Everybody's head turned toward Jason who was sitting in the back row with Jackson and Cassie. He was slumped down in his chair, his legs stretched far in front of him, his hands folded in his lap, and his eyes pointed to the floor. He didn't even look up. Right now Brad felt like an idiot opening this up with Jason here. He thought it was going to be a good idea, giving the kids a chance to have some input, and learn a little about what was happening rather then being in the dark. They all knew there were problems, and he didn't want their imaginations filling in the blanks.

"No. Some people got some misinformation, and jumped to conclusions on that information."

Another hand came up. "Is he going to quit?"

"Pastor Knoll?" Brad asked. "I don't know. I don't think so, but I don't know. I hope not."

"Why were you guys arrested?"

That question caught Brad off-guard. He didn't want to trash Jerry, but he needed to make it clear to these kids that he hadn't been arrested.

"You know, that picture wasn't quite correct. Somebody started yelling at me in the hospital, trying to fight me, and Pastor Knoll came over and broke us up. The police showed up then and the other guy took off. That's when they took the picture, so it's a little misleading."

"Did you know the guy?"

"Yeah."

"Who was it?"

"I'm not gonna tell you that."

"Ah man. Come on, Brad."

"No."

"I bet you could have taken him if Pastor hadn't jumped in though. Huh?"

Everyone busted up laughing at that. Seeing Brad fighting at a hospital was just too much.

Gerry raised her hand then, and Brad called on her.

"Is next Sunday really your last Sunday?"

"Next Sunday? Where did you hear that?"

"Around. Is it?" Gerry sounded so grown up. So angry. She had changed immensely since camp. He really felt bad for her, he couldn't imagine the inner struggle she must be going through, between her parents and her friends.

"Not that I've heard. Not by my choice anyway. I guess I could get fired, but then we would just have to have fifth quarters at my house."

"Man, they better not fire you." That sentence sparked a lot of loud verbal agreement. It made Brad feel good. He loved these kids so much, and to feel the love they had for him was amazing.

"Hey guys, listen. I might be fired I might not. Nevertheless, my authority to teach you, and my love for you isn't given to me by the Community Church of Lendel. They just sign my paychecks. It is God that has given me the desire to teach you guys, and He's the One who placed me here, and no one is getting rid of me unless God says its time. They may be able to take away our room, my office, even my financial support, but they can't take away my choice to teach. We are in a war here. I don't mean necessarily at just this church, but Christians in general. My generation and the generation before me dropped the ball. We've allowed too much influence from the world into our churches and teaching, we've compromised doctrines in the name of keeping peace, we have failed to give your generation the necessary tools to fight, to stand, because we've been to afraid we'd drive you away. We wanted to share the freedom in Christ, and we've actually enslaved you in the lack of knowledge, and the ability to discern right from wrong. We've blurred the line of black and white, and created just a light shade of gray that allows each to interpret the gospel however they 'feel' it should be, to fit there lifestyle. We've allowed people to say 'this is what I think it means' or that the Bible is for personal interpretation. That is the antithesis of what the Bible says. In fact, who has a Bible…Jackson?…Turn to Second Peter. I think near the end of chapter one. Sorry guys I'm getting a little off the subject but this is really important. Okay, yeah, here it is, 'Knowing this first, that no prophecy of the scripture is of any private interpretation. For the prophecy came not in old time by the will of man: but the holy men of God spoke as they were moved by the Holy Ghost.' See you can't bend it to what you want. Scripture says what it says. The dude from the Supertones hits this right on the head. They have this song called Grounded, I'm sure most of you have heard it, it says: 'War rages on through generations. All of these Christians abandoned their stations. A whole world around us that we've ceased to reach. An army of soldiers we've neglected to teach.' That's you guys." Brad said pointing across the room. He continued. "Kid's in universities, drowning in an ocean of apostate philosophy, we need apologetic instruction, mental reconstruction, Ignorance reduction, to halt the mass abduction. Evangelical minds have been scandalized, wisdom and truth have been vandalized, by the unevangelized.' This is where we get a little hope. 'But its dim and not pitch black, the truth will prevail. If our God is for us, how can we fail?' Now my job is to give you guys the weapons you need to be able to stand. I have to ground you guys in the scriptures. So no, I'm not going to leave."

The room was silent, there were a few tears, and then a little sniffle. A tall, very slender boy stood up in the back row. His name was Alan Bennet. He was extremely quiet, shy, in fact Brad had never heard him talk in front of more than one or two people.

"I'm ready to stand." He said firmly. Those four words made a bigger impact then the last three hundred Brad had just spoke.

Nobody even turned to look back at him, but they all began standing. One or two at first, then all. They were all standing. Times like this made everything he had gone through completely worth it. They remained at the church for another two hours, praying for the deacons, each other, but most of all, for Pastor Knoll.

Brad pulled into his drive, noticing only the porch light and a lamp in the living room were on. He glanced down at the time on his radio. 11:11. *Make a wish.* That was Jenny's favorite saying. He hoped that Jenny had fallen asleep and not worried too much. He had forgotten to call and let her know they were running late.

He worked his key quietly in the lock, and pulled up on the door knob as he swung it open to step inside. It didn't seem to creak as loud when he lifted it like that. He took off his coat and hung it on the coat rack. Trying to tiptoe down the hall, he didn't notice the 'singing doll' located directly in front of him. He kicked it and the song went off.

"Twinkle, twinkle, little star…"

Brad pounced on the doll trying to smother the sound. The doll finally ended, but now Brad was stuck. If he got up the pressure release would cause the doll to start singing again, and he was laying on top of his hands which were no where near the off switch. He made up his mind. He would roll over onto his back, squeezing the doll with one hand, he would free the other to turn it off. It was now or never. Brad rolled quickly, freed his right hand, everything was going perfect until he realized the off switch was against his body. The doll won. Brad had to let it go but he got it shut off before the second twinkle. He got to his feet and turned to head down the hall. As soon as he turned, he jumped ten inches off the ground. Jenny was standing right in front of him, her hands resting on her belly, laughing harder than he had ever seen her laugh before. He started to say something but couldn't think of anything that could save him from this embarrassment.

"So what did the doll say to make you mad? Or did it give you 'that look'?" It took Jenny five minutes to get those two short sentences out. She could barely breathe, let alone talk.

"What? I can't even understand you?" Brad was starting to get tickled now too.

"It probably smarted off to you didn't it. I know how you hate that."

"C'mon, I didn't want to wake you up."

Jenny didn't say anything in return. She had quit laughing but was still doubled over, her teeth biting hard on her bottom lip. She looked up at him slowly, her eyes wide in fear.

"I (huh, huh) think my (huh, huh) water just broke."

Chapter 12

James breathed a sigh of relief as he watched the headlights flood his living room. It was only 10:30 but he had told Jason to be home at ten. Jason had never been late and always called even if he thought he was going to be a little late.

He heard the front door open up and headed to the foyer to meet Jason.

"Where have you been? We were worried to death!"

"The fifth quarter ran late. I had to leave early to get Cassie home without being in trouble. Sorry."

"That's alright. You should have called though." James had no reason not to believe him.

"Hey Dad, I got a question."

"Shoot."

"Are you gonna quit?"

This took James completely by surprise. He didn't know exactly how to respond. He really hadn't wanted to answer it.

"What do you mean?"

"I mean quit preaching. Here."

"I don't know Jace. I don't want to, but I might not have a choice."

"So you're just gonna give up. You're just gonna quit. I can't believe you." Tears were welling up in Jason's eyes.

"No son, I'm not giving up. I might not have a choice. This isn't about me, it's deeper than that. If this was just a job, or I cared more about having a nice comfortable house in a nice comfortable town, than I did the people in the town, then I would just preach cushy, lovey-dovey, 'how could I make you feel good about your sins' sermons. But I don't. I could also force the church into a 'pastor confidence' vote and I imagine I would get the majority, then give the others the opportunity to either leave or change. What does that say to the community? Whether people like to admit it or not, this church is a landmark in our community. People look up to it. We are an example to this community, and people know where we stand. What are they going to think about Christianity when they see us like this? My reputation has been trashed, but I'm not as worried about what people think of me, but what they think of the pastor. I'm not giving up, God may just be saying 'it's time for you to move on'. I talked to your grandfather today, and that's what he said. "It might be time for you to move on son." He is the only person who has given me that advice. Everyone else has said to fight them, to strike at them from the pulpit. I can't do that son. I would like to stay, but I don't honestly know if I will be able to."

Jason was standing there looking at him. He was fighting back his tears so hard. They were right there ready to burst.

"If you left where would you go?"

"Oh man Jason, I don't know? I haven't even looked. Right now, I'm not planning on going anywhere, I'm just not going to lie to you. I might. I'm not planning on it, I'm not candidating, and I'm not looking. I'm focused on right here, right now."

"I'm sorry dad. I love you." Jason said falling into his dads arms letting the tears flow free.

"I love you too, Jace. I love you too."

* * * *

"Shouldn't you have been having some stronger contractions first." Brad said as he wove in and out of the traffic.

"I don't know Brad, I've never done this before. Haunggggg. They're coming pretty strong now." She was lifting herself up off the seat with both her hands, locking her elbows and straightening her legs.

"Man I'm excited."

"Yeah. Ahhhhhh.(huh, huh). Me too."

Brad screeched his car to a stop right in front of the ER door. He jumped out running around their car to help her out. The EMT's were right there with a wheelchair. Jenny slid in softly bracing herself for the ride. She was imagining a ride like what she saw on television. She expected them to be running her, in the chair, down the hall with the doctor rushing behind them, screaming orders and complaining because her room wasn't ready. She was surprised.

Brad was trying to create a sense of urgency in the wheelchair operator, who seemed to be taking extra long. He was the slow car in the fast lane with his blinker on to scare anyone from passing, just in case. Finally, they reached the Maternity Ward. He pushed her to the front desk and left her there in the hands of the receptionist. Jenny would have been worried if she hadn't been in so much pain.

"So did you guys pre-register?"

"Yes, three weeks ago. Where's Dr. Gray?" Brad's excitement was written all over his face.

The receptionist giggled a bit. "Probably home in bed. It's 11:40."

"At Home! We're having a baby don't you think he should be here?" Jenny screamed.

"It's okay Mrs. Howe. He'll be here when its time. Now, did you guys pick a room when you pre-registered?"

"No." Brad wasn't paying much attention to the receptionist he was busy watching his wife's face contort with each contraction. They were coming about three minutes apart, and Brad's excitement was growing at the same rate.

"Okay then I'll go ahead and buzz the nurse and we'll get your room all set up for you." She smiled a genuine smile, then pressed a button on a large board.

It wasn't long before a short, almost round nurse came bustling down the hall. She was wearing scrubs with storks all over them. She seemed so happy and helpful, even from a glance, and she was.

"Ooohh, I'm so excited. Is this your first?"

"Yes." Came the response in surround sound.

"That's always the funnest. Now just relax…" She started down the hall with Jenny leaving Brad behind with all the bags. Brad watched them walk into a room on the left, turning in himself when he got there.

"As soon as you put those bags down, you get over here and rub her shoulders. She needs to relax."

Brad smiled, and set the bags on the ground. It was funny, she didn't seem as bossy as she was, and Brad didn't mind that she hadn't even talked to him at all except to tell him what to do. She was completely concerned with Jenny and that was all that mattered to him. Nurse Ann, as she wanted to be called, reminded him more and more of Maiden Marian's nurse-maid in the Robin Hood Tales. Especially the cartoon version. She looked, talked, moved, and acted just like Clucky, the hen.

He began rubbing Jenny's shoulders, he could feel all her muscles tighten with each contraction. He felt so bad for her, he had never seen her in this kind of pain and Nurse Ann had assured them that 'this was nothing'. He hated to see what was in store. He kept wondering what their baby was going to look like. Even what it was going to be, boy or girl.

"Thanks for rubbing honey. Maybe you should go call mom and dad, and the Knoll's."

"Oh yeah I almost forgot. Can I use the phone in this room?"

"Why yes. It's yours." Nurse Ann shook her head smiling.

Brad tuned out as soon as he got Jenny's mom on the phone. He was going crazy on the phone, ecstatic. Jenny was more low-keyed. Nervous.

"Shouldn't my doctor be here?"

"Oh he will be honey. You still have a couple hours to go. Which reminds me, I need to check you real quick."

It wasn't long until parents and pastor were there, driving the excitement level in the hospital up about 20%. Jenny wasn't making much progress, she had dilated to five quickly but had been stuck there for three hours. Finally, Nurse Ann suggested they get some sleep. Brad didn't think he could fall asleep but it took him only fifteen minutes. Jenny fell in and out of sleep throughout the night. Nurse Ann continued to check her and tried to make her as comfortable as possible. The families and friends all stayed in the waiting room.

Brad was jerked from sleep with a scream. He rolled off the bed not knowing where he was. He saw the clock and was having a difficult time figuring out what time it was. He knew the big hand was on the three, but he couldn't make right in his mind if the little hand was on the five or six. His head eventually cleared and he saw it on the five. Another scream/growl and he jumped to his feet.

"GET-A-NURSE-NOW!!!"

Brad flew out of the room, sliding around the corner. He saw Nurse Ann waddling down the hall.

"Is everything alright?"

"NO. Jenny's going crazy."

"Well let's go see what's going on."

The patience that had been a comfort earlier in the evening was annoying the urgent Brad now.

It didn't take her long to get fired up, once she checked Jenny this time. She came rushing out of their room throwing orders around, getting the machines in the room and set up, and finally calling the doctor. She was gone only about five minutes and came back in the room completely ready to deliver their baby. She got Jenny pushing and Brad coaching, and by the time the doctor got there, the baby had crowned.

"I can see its head, I can see its head." Brad was screaming at Jenny who was completely exhausted and could barely push. This did excite her and gave her a second wind.

Jenny mustered up the last bit of energy she had and gave a tremendous push. She pushed the face out and two more pushes the baby slid into the doctor's arms.

"It's a girl. Honey, it's a girl. Madeline. Madeline." Tears were streaming down Brads face, he looked back and forth between Madeline and his wife torn between which he should stay with. He decided to follow the nurses with their new baby girl. He was watching them wipe her off, measure her, clean out her lungs, but he couldn't hear Jenny saying anything. All of a sudden, he got extremely scared. He rushed over to her side, and grabbed her hand. Her face looked pale, and her eyes looked like no one was inside. He kissed her forehead.

"Is she okay doc?"

"I'm fine, Brad." Jenny's voice was very quiet. "Stay with Madeline, please. Can I hold her yet?"

"Not yet." Nurse Ann had overheard them talking.

"Should I go tell them yet?"

"No. I want to hold her before everyone comes in."

"Here you go." Nurse Ann turned Madeline over to her mom.

Jenny's tears rolled down her face, soaking her pillow. She kept stroking her head and whispering, "You're so beautiful. So beautiful."

The nurses finally took Madeline to get her washed and all the other necessities, and Jenny got some much needed rest. Brad stayed with the nurses, holding up his new baby girl for all the grandparents, by blood or proxy, to see. There was cheering and tears in the waiting room outside the nursery.

* * * *

Bill stared at the paper in front of him. He was having second thoughts about signing it, but he really didn't have much choice. He had gotten in so deep, he couldn't turn back. If he quit now, he knew they wouldn't let him out. Well not without taking something from him. He took a deep breath and closed his eyes. He made a decision, the best decision for his family, or so he thought. He signed his name to the bottom, and put his stamp on the blank space. He had been told that this was the last one he had to do and for that he was relieved. Granted, it had helped at the time, they had gotten into debt that they couldn't afford, and they needed the extra money. Now, they had paid those loans off and got involved in an investment with Adam and were making plenty of money. He had rationalized it at the time, reminding himself of all he had done for the company, and the overtime he had worked and not got paid for, he had even thought, *they're a multimillion dollar company, what's twenty or thirty grand.* It wasn't like he was stealing outright, he had authorized payment on some work for a friend of his, that wasn't needed and never done, and they split the money when he got paid. *It's not my fault no one checked up on the work. If I hadn't done this someone else would've and taken them for a lot more. They're lucky it was me.*

He sealed the paper in an envelope, and placed it in his out box. He had to get ready for their meeting tonight, so he needed to make some calls. He decided to try Jerry's house first. No answer. Next, he tried Adam's, no answer there either. He needed to talk with someone. He couldn't just sit there, he was too nervous, he kept thinking about what he had been doing. What would happen if he ever got caught?

He decided to call his dad. Henry Peters was planning on joining them tonight for their prayer meeting, it was the first time in three months that he had come to any of these. He hadn't even been to church in about four weeks. He had skipped all his trustee meetings, but hadn't yet resigned. Bill and Henry didn't talk too much about all the things going on in their church, their opinions differed on some things, but they did agree on several. One of these was that Pastor Knoll had to go. *Huh, no answer. I wonder where he's at?*

Bill caught himself biting his nails. He pulled them back from his face to look at them. He had chewed most of them down to the quick. He had never chewed his nails until about two or three months ago, but now if he wasn't eating or chewing sunflower seeds, he had his finger tips in his mouth.

Chapter 13

"Yeah, she weighed 8lbs. 5oz."

"Wow. Are they going to bring her to church Sunday?"

"Who?" Jerry asked, walking into the room, catching the end of their conversation.

"Madeline. Brad and Jenny's new baby." Gerry said excitedly.

"Oh. Hey, are you guys gonna go somewhere tonight while we have our meeting?" Jerry replied turning his attention toward his wife.

"I guess, if you need us to."

"Yeah it would probably be best."

"What are you guys talking about tonight?"

"You'll see soon enough. I'm gonna go watch Sports Center, let me know when you leave alright."

"Alright." Pam turned back to the computer she had been working on, and Gerry headed upstairs to her room.

Pam's frustration was growing, and whether Jerry knew it or not he was losing her. She had always looked up to him so much, but now she almost couldn't stand to be in the same room as him. She tried to talk, she tried to engage in activities he enjoyed, she was making his favorite foods, and still no response. He didn't talk except to tell, he was overly concerned with the deacons. He continued blowing off Gerry every time she said anything to him, and was being far too lax with Rachel. He allowed her to get away with almost anything, and made excuses for all her actions. Pam's family was falling apart before her eyes.

Pam's church family was falling apart also, and as little as Jerry wanted to talk to her about their personal problems, he was even more unwilling to discuss anything with her about the church. They totally disagreed with what was going on, so they skipped that topic as much as possible. She would leave tonight, and she would go visit Brad and Jenny in the hospital. In fact, she would charge the nicest gift she could find on his credit card. *Maybe a crib, or a real nice car seat.* She was trying to think of the things they had already and she couldn't remember a crib. *That's what I think I'll get. A crib. One of the nice wooden ones. Not a plastic or vinyl one. In fact, I think I'll get the extra thick mattress to go along with it. And Jerry will just have to like it.* Thinking of this cheered her up a bit.

She went upstairs to talk to Gerry and see if she wanted to go with her.

"Sure. What time are we gonna leave, so I can get ready?"

"Get ready? We're just going to the hospital."

"Well I need to at least change clothes. And we need to get a gift don't we?" "Yeah. Adam and those guys are coming over in about an hour, so I figured we'd leave in about 45 minutes."

"Okay, I'll be ready. Hey mom, are they going to try to get rid of Brad?"

"Who honey?" Pam asked already knowing the answer.

"Dad and those guys. Why do they hate him so much?"

"They don't hate him honey, they, well they feel uncomfortable with him. They have some issues with Pastor Knoll, and so I guess they throw Brad into the mix as well. I don't think you need to worry about Brad. God will take care of him."

"So they are trying to get rid of him."

"No, I don't think so."

"They better not."

Pam smiled and left the room to get ready herself. She could hear the refrigerator door open and Jerry rustling through the food. She thought about going down there, but gave up the idea.

Where in the world did she put the creamer. Jerry was looking for the Irish Cream he had bought yesterday, to add flavor to his coffee. He had been meeting Adam at a coffee shop downtown and had fallen in love with the Irish Cream Cappuccinos. He finally found it, stirred it into his coffee and headed to the den for the second half of Sports Center. He sat down in his chair and sipped his warm coffee. The flavor brought back memories from just last night. At first he thought of Adam, and then thought of them at the volleyball game, and finally of Candy. The first time she popped into his mind he always tried pushing it away, but then she would come right back. His imagination continued bringing up situations that would force them together. Tragedies to their family, them getting stuck some where, irresistible attraction. The sound of Sports Center pulled him back to reality, but each time his mind wandered it was gone for longer, and longer. The flag of lust was slowly replacing the flag of paranoia in his heart and mind.

"I'm leaving honey." Jerry heard Pam's voice ringing down the hall.

"Alright. We'll probably get done pretty late."

"Okay, we'll be home late too. Love you, bye."

"Bye."

She couldn't even kiss me bye. Jerry had noticed they never kissed bye anymore. They never kissed hi. They never kissed. Their paths seldom crossed and this made him sad. He wished they could spend more time together, and after all this was over, he would. He would be able to take time for her and the girls, but right now, he was so busy with his business, his corporation with Adam, and all the stuff going on at the church it was just too much. *She understands* he kept telling himself.

He heard the door close and went into the kitchen to make some fresh coffee. He poured out the nearly full pot of coffee he had just made and started a new one. The door bell rang, so he put the coffee back in the lazy-susan and headed to the door. He could tell when he stepped into the foyer that it was Jack. He could see his bald head with the 3 strands of hair combed from the left side of his head across to the right. Jack was standing there in his thick wool coat with the collars pulled high on his neck, his shoulders shrugged. Jerry hurried to the door not wanting to leave his new friend out in the cold.

"Jack, come on in." Jack stomped his feet as if there was snow on them. There wasn't. Jerry closed the door behind him.

"Man, it's gettin' cold too soon. I didn't think my car was ever gonna warm up on the way over here."

"We've been cranking the heat this whole week. We need to start the wood stove but I've been too lazy to get the wood."

"We fired up ours last night. It was kinda nice. It reminded me of when the kids used ta be home." Jack's eyes were filling up with tears. "Those were some great times."

Jerry was looking at the older man's eyes. They were moist, and he was blinking hard. He put his large rough hand up to his face and wiped away the single tear squeezed out by his eyelid.

"Is something wrong Jack?" Jerry knew there had to be, Jack was a tough old man who came from the school of thought that, 'men don't cry'.

Jack shook his head. "Na, jist gettin' a little sentimental, I guess." He looked back up at Jerry and his eyes were dry. "Do ya think I could get somethin' ta drink?"

"Oh sure. Um, we got coffee, water and I think maybe some hot chocolate."

"I'll take a cup of coffee."

Jerry poured himself and Jack a cup, his touched off with creamer, and they headed into the den. One by one, the other men started wandering in. Bill and Henry Peters, who rode together, came first, then Ben right after, followed by Mark, and Adam finally showed up twenty minutes late. As soon as he showed up, everyone turned to him to guide their meeting. Even Jerry who had been leading it, turned the authority to him.

"Well, as you know, we have a situation with Pastor Knoll. I have talked to several of you about what I think we should do, but I want to know what YOU think we should do." Everyone was quiet. "Bill, what do you think?"

"Well at first I just wanted to talk it out with Pastor, but now, after listening to more people my mind is starting to change. I don't know that we can talk to him. I think what we need to do is tell him what we expect, and if he can't live with it, then tough."

Jerry sat there quietly. He had given a lot of thought this week to what they should do. He was going to tell everyone what he thought but he was going to wait until everyone was heard from first.

"But what do you expect?" Adam was guiding him into his answers like a politician at a convention with his pre-appointed questions.

"I expect him to be concerned about the people that have been leaving. I expect him to not be so hard on everyone, show a little more love. I expect him not to get angry, not to be so close-minded, willing to listen."

"What if he doesn't listen to you?"

"Then we ask him to resign." Bill sounded like he was reading from a Teleprompter.

"Well, you sound pretty sure. How about you Mark?"

"I think we just ought to get rid of him. We are going to have a hard time getting anyone to work with him. I also think we should consider asking Brad to resign."

"I don't think we should go that far." Ben spoke up quickly. "I think IF Pastor Knoll leaves Brad would probably leave too. But I don't think we should even consider getting rid of him. He is the best youth pastor this church has ever had."

"I agree with Ben, we shouldn't get rid of Brad, he'll probably leave on his own, after Pastor Knoll leaves. Plus, I don't want to make all the teen's parents mad. You all know how I feel about James though. I haven't liked him from the beginning. So I'm all for asking him to resign." Everyone pretty much knew what Jack was going to say before hand.

"Henry, what do you think?"

"I honestly don't know. I've heard everything from Bill and Ben, but I've also talked to Phillip. I don't exactly know what I think."

"That's fair. How about you Jerry?"

"Well, I'm glad you asked. I've been giving it a lot of thought." Jerry stood up. "I think maybe we should take it in front of the church. Now I know I have been dead set against it in the past but I think with a decision this big the whole church needs to be involved. I think so far we have done a good job of decision making, but this is too big. I don't know what would happen, if we would decide to keep him, or ship him, but I think we should leave the decision up to the church."

"You know Jerry, I completely agree with you. I think we should allow the church to decide, but I think we need to present both sides of the story. I think we should let James make a case for himself, and then I think we should give one of us a chance at a rebuttal. Then the people would be able to make an informed decision."

Jerry was feeling pretty good about himself now. He had brought an idea to the table and Adam agreed. He really felt like they were making the right decision.

Bill chimed in with his agreement. "We should tell James Friday at the deacon's meeting. We also need to get a hold of everyone and make sure they are there Sunday."

Everyone seemed to agree, so the meeting ended earlier than everyone expected. Ben was the first to leave. He gave Henry a ride home since Bill and Adam wanted to stay and talk for awhile. Jack and Mark left quickly afterward. Jerry walked them to the door, and then refreshed Adam and Bill's coffee.

"So how's the mill treating you, Bill?" Jerry didn't really care he was just trying to talk about something other than the church.

"Pretty good. I've been swamped with work lately, and haven't had much time for anything else. I'm looking forward to getting this thing settled at the church, so I'll at least have some free time."

"I know what you mean. Between this and the dry cleaners I don't even have time to watch the World Series." Jerry shook his head.

"Then we need to make sure it's over this Sunday." Adam sounded cold. "You guys don't need to be suffering, and neither do your families. Don't you see what he is doing to us? We need to be ready on Sunday, we need to make sure the right people are there and are ready to talk. We need to make sure he can't weasel his way out." "What do you mean the right people?"

"I mean like Mark, and Jack, even you Jerry. Didn't he try to fight you?"

"Well no, not exactly."

"But he would have if you had continued towards Brad, don't you think?"

"Maybe, probably, I don't know."

"Do you really think a Pastor should take physical action against a deacon?"

"No. But…Never mind."

"What?"

"Well don't you think Mark might embellish the truth a little?"

"No. I mean the only people that know the truth are him and James, and you know James will lie to save his skin."

"Another thing Jerry, is that whether we like it or not, James' picture in the paper with the police, has really hurt this church. He hasn't even tried to explain why he was in it. I don't even know. We have to make a change."

Bill had made a good point. Jerry's past with James had made its last stand, and just like Custer, it lost. His mind was made at that moment, he would do whatever it took to get rid of James.

* * * *

James squeezed his wife's hand as they came out of the restaurant, heading to their car. The dinner had been great and it was really nice talking with Robert and Denise. Robert had gotten a baby sitter for the night and had come up to take his parents to dinner. They had talked about Jason, and their boys, and Robert's church, but avoided what was going on here. James knew that they wanted to know, but he didn't want to worry them about the problems here, or give them any reason to plant some sort of bitterness in their hearts toward churches in general.

"So how are you doin' dad?"

"Good. This week has been nice. Not a single crisis." James laughed. "Just a new baby."

"Oh yeah. Isn't she beautiful? After Robert and I saw her it really made me want a girl."

"Yeah she was pretty. Jason called me, and said you are thinking about leaving." Robert said, changing the subject.

"No. I said I *might* leave, but right now, we aren't thinking about moving. This week has been really nice. I mean right now it's Thursday and I only have a deacon's meeting tomorrow. I've had no calls complaining, or worried, or problems. It's been nice. I think things might be settling down, and headed up." He patted Hannah on her knee. "So, where you guys going to Youth Camp this year?"

"Well we're going to the winter camp Brad started, and I think we are going to go on a mission trip instead, this summer."

"That'll be pretty neat. Where to?"

"Probably Peru. The Collins are missionaries there, and we thought we would help them. They are the ones our youth group has been supporting." Robert and James continued talking about youth camps and retreats, while Hannah and Denise talked about granddaughters.

They finally made it to their house in time to watch the third game of the World Series. While James and Robert headed for the T.V., Denise and Hannah decided to go by and see Jenny and Madeline again.

"I think we should stop by the store and get a gift, maybe grab them something to eat too." Denise was talking excitedly.

"That's a good idea. Do you guys want to go along?" Hannah yelled back to her boys in the T.V. room.

"No!"

Hannah heard them start laughing.

"No thanks honey. I think we're gonna stay and watch the game."

Hannah and Denise headed into the room to say bye.

"See you guys later."

"Alright. Hey could you pick me up a candy bar or something?" James always ate a candy bar when he watched sports. It had turned into a habit.

"Sure. We won't be back for a while though."

"Oh yeah. Hey, have Jace drop one by when he leaves Brad's."

"Okay, if he's still there when we get there. Do you want anything Robert?"

"No thanks mom."

"See you guys."

Chapter 14

Brad pulled out of the drive-thru, unwrapping the burger he had just bought. He wasn't looking forward to the meeting tonight, but he wasn't dreading it as usual. He had been so preoccupied with his new daughter he hadn't had much time to think about the problems with their church.

He bit into his burger and immediately vowed he would never eat there again. The last three times he had ordered something they had made it wrong. He hated pickles, had asked for no pickles, saw 'no pickles' pop up on the courtesy screen, and yet his burger was packed with pickles. *I should take it back.* He glanced down at his clock and realized he didn't have enough time. It was 7:20 and their meeting started in ten minutes. He decided to just pick them off knowing that he would still be able to taste pickle juice.

He rolled down his window to toss them out. He felt the cold wind rush in, cutting through his skin like a knife. It was only October and the wind chill was already six below. That was strange, this area was called the banana belt of Colorado, they were only supposed to have two or three months of cold weather and October wasn't one of them.

His anger over the pickles subsided as his hunger pains grew less. He started wandering about what was going to happen at the meeting tonight. Maybe it was Madeline getting here, or him being preoccupied with her birth, but for some reason this week had kind of reminded him of how it used to be. No fighting, no bickering, things seemed to be a lot smoother. Maybe everyone had gotten over their hang-ups.

He pulled up to the church and right away noticed how few cars were there. Only Pastor Knoll's and Jacks. *That's got be an uncomfortable situation.* Brad laughed a little. He knew Jack was probably more uncomfortable than James.

Brad parked his car and headed into the church. He almost got knocked over by James office door opening up. Jack and James stepped out, Jack with tears streaming down his face. Brad being there scared Jack and he jumped, quickly wiping away the tears.

"I'm gittin' too old, Brad." Jack said with a pat on Brad's shoulder as he passed by him towards the bathroom.

"What was that all about?" Brad asked James.

"Oh nothing. I'll talk to you about it later." He put his arm around Brad's shoulders and headed toward the stairs. "Let's go get ready for the meeting. I think we're going to get a lot of stuff settled tonight."

"Yeah, me too."

It wasn't long before everyone started showing up and the meeting got underway. There was some talk of general business at first, then finally Jerry made a motion.

"I'd like to make a motion that we go ahead and bring all our questions about James to the church."

"I'd like to second that." Bill added quickly.

"Wait a minute." James was wary of this, since he had wanted it for so long and they had been set against it. "What are we going to bring before the church?"

"I just think that it is time we are open and honest about what has been going on. We need to let the people speak, and if the people are for you then everyone needs to shut up and leave you alone. If the people are against you however, we would like you to make the decision God would lead you to make."

"How much percentage does he need?" Jack asked.

"Just the majority. I don't think we need to say 80% or 75%, just the majority. Does everyone think that's fair?"

A lot of heads were nodding in agreement with Jerry.

"Okay then. Is that alright with you Pastor?"

"Yes, that's fine."

James was pretty happy. He knew the majority of the people would side with him, probably around 85-90% and he was glad Jerry had changed his attitude. He was unguarded however, to the trap that had been set. It was the wolf in sheep's clothing. He was so happy that the deacons hearts appeared to have changed he wasn't even looking for the ambush. It was a perfectly designed plan and if executed properly it could destroy James life. If he walked into the auditorium Sunday, unprepared for the attacks against him, his morale would be completely wiped out. It could destroy his ability to ever effectively minister again.

They continued for about a half hour, going on with the typical business of their meetings, everyone in a jovial mood. All because of the same thing, but for very different reasons. When they finally dismissed, everyone left right away. There was no one staying around afterward in their little groups, gossiping about one another, they all just got up and went home. James felt such a sense of relief over what was happening. In two days it would all be settled. He couldn't wait to get home and tell Hannah. He drove up Skyline Drive to thank God for what had happened.

Hannah was waiting by the door when James got home.

"So. How was it?"

"Well I have some bad news and some good news. Which do you want to hear first?"

"Well usually I say the bad so this time…The good."

"The deacons have had a change of heart. They've decided to let the church decide, so this Sunday we're going to have a vote."

"Wow, almost everyone in the church wants you to stay, don't they?"

"Well I think the majority. You know what else?"

"What?"

"Adam wasn't there. I don't know where he was at, but he hasn't missed a meeting since probably July. It was nice, finally having a meeting with just Brad and the deacons."

"This is great. So what's the bad news?"

"Well, Jack Johnson came early and wanted to talk to me. He went to the doctor last week and they sent him to the hospital in

Denver. Anyway, I guess he has liver cancer."

"Oh my goodness. Is he going to have to start chemo or something?"

"Actually, the cancer is too advanced. They said he could try some different treatments, but they would only give him about a 10% chance for survival. The doctors gave him three months to live."

"Three months? He doesn't look sick. How's Janice?"

"He hasn't told her yet. He went to the doctor while she was visiting Brenda in Kansas. He doesn't want her to know, because he's afraid she'll worry, and try to get him treatment, which will just give her false hope. He said he has known he was dying for the last year, and that this was just the confirmation. He also apologized for all the problems he had caused, and now he knows what it is like to have a cancer. He still remembers Phillip calling him that and he says he thinks he was. He was feeding off the weakness and problems we had. He was living by trying to destroy me and the more damage he could cause the bigger he felt. He said that it's just like the cancer in him. It lives by killing."

"Jack said all that?"

"Yeah. He broke into tears several times, and asked for my forgiveness. I hugged him, I didn't think he was ever going to let me go. And then he told me…" James started to tear up. "He told me he loved me."

Hannah started crying then too. "This makes it all worth it. Maybe this is why we went through all this, to get to this point with Jack."

James just shook his head. He was happy to have a new friend, and sad he would be losing him soon.

Just then, the phone rang. James dried his tears and cleared his throat.

"Hello."

"James. Hi, this is Jack."

* * * *

Jerry's lights reflected off the back off Bill's truck. He had stopped to fill up with gas before heading over to Adam's. Bill, Mark and him were meeting at Adam's after the deacon's meeting to discuss their strategy for Sunday morning. Jerry had some ideas and he had imagined them out in his mind. He had even imagined it breaking out in violence, and him having to save Candy's life. He would rush her away from there and they would later get the call of his wife's and Adam's death. Every time he thought of this, he felt a tinge of guilt. He didn't really want his wife to die, he loved her more than anything, he just had this lustful desire for Candy.

Jerry rang the doorbell and Candy answered it.

"Jerry, I'm glad you made it." She said giving him a big hug.

His face turned bright red and he hugged her back, not wanting to let go. Adam came in the foyer,

"Jerry. I was getting worried about you. Everyone else has been here for twenty minutes. I thought maybe you had gotten in a wreck or something."

"No I just had to get some gas."

Just then, Jerry realized his arm was still around Candy who was trying to move over to Adam. His face turned red again and pulled his arm from around her waist.

They headed into the living room and Jerry saw everyone there already nestled in their chairs. He moved over to the couch and Adam brought him out a cup of coffee.

"Well, what we were thinking about, is having a prayer meeting during Sunday School for everyone who wants to come. I figured a lot of the people will want to come to that and maybe we can get a chance to talk to some of them. Then everyone will know we are wanting to do what is best, and not just out on a vendetta against James." Adam continued. "We need to make sure and let James go first, he'll feel comfortable and won't say anything harsh. He might not even try to defend himself. Then I think Mark should go."

"Who is going to be in charge of this whole thing?" Bill asked.

"Well, we'll need to vote in a moderator first thing. I think it would be good if we had either Ben, or Hank. They can kinda run the show from there. After Mark gives his talk, Jerry you should go next. You need to say whatever is on your heart. Then, I met this guy named Ty Castle. I guess he met James when he first moved here about 7 years ago. James did some things that you all would be amazed at. Ty was there with him, so he's going to talk after Jerry."

"Ty? What did he see? What'd they do?"

"You'll see on Sunday. I promise you'll be surprised. We also need to make sure that this is on the radio. I imagine James will want to broadcast a taped sermon, but the people of Lendel need to know what is going on."

"What happens if he gets the majority?" Bill asked.

"He won't. Not after Mark, Jerry and Ty speak. There is no way."

"How do you know that Ty is going to tell the truth. How do you know he told you the truth?" Jerry was feeling uneasy about this mysterious Ty fellow.

"He has no reason to lie."

Chapter 15

James felt such a peace about today. He had been excited for it early Friday, had been dreading it yesterday, but today he just felt a peace. He had pulled up to the church early as usual, and turned the heat on in the sanctuary. He saw about fifteen cars there when he arrived which was very strange. He usually spent about half an hour studying and praying in his office before the first Sunday school teachers started showing up. He had passed by the men and women gathered in the prayer room on the way to his office. He glanced in but continued down the hall. It was almost completely full by the time Sunday school started. James didn't teach a class so he just stayed in his office praying and reading and preparing. The church service was about to begin. They would have about fifteen minutes of congregational singing, then the deacons had asked him to go ahead and speak first. He didn't know exactly what he was going to say, or even what he should say, he was relying on God for that. God promised he would supply our every need, and words were James' number one need now.

James saw the flood of kids rushing down the hall, the certain sign that Sunday School was over. He took a deep breath trying to clear his mind, then stepped into the hall. He noticed the door to the prayer room was still closed, and he passed by it on his way to the auditorium. He started to open one of the doors when he saw Brad, and the entire youth department, kneeling on the stage, praying. He loved Brad and was grateful to have him on staff all these years. The church people didn't know how blessed they were to have him teaching their children. The group on stage slowly got up, signaling the end of their prayer meeting. Soon after, the piano began playing its welcoming tune, and people started filing in to the auditorium.

James felt the pats on the back and heard the "Morning Pastor" as he walked toward the front. He usually loved Sunday mornings, seeing friends, saying hi to all the visitors and especially seeing the kids. Today though, he felt distant. He went up front to the pew he always sat in. Hannah was there waiting for him. He sat down beside her and she slid her arm around his waist.

"I love you honey." She whispered in his ear.

"I love you too."

He pressed his hands on his knees, took a deep breath, filling his chest, and straightened his back against the pew.

"Are you ready?"

"I guess I have to be."

The song service flew by faster than James had expected. Next thing he knew Jerry was walking towards the front. He stepped up on stage and made his way to the pulpit. He adjusted the microphone down to fit his stature.

"I believe most of you know what is happening today and trust you have been praying for us. We had a prayer meeting this morning and asked God to guide us in our decisions today. I trust that each of you will put aside all prejudices and past memories to be completely open to what you hear today. Before we begin this morning, I think it would be wise if we motion someone in as a moderator. I am not anticipating any bad behavior but just to be on the safe side I think we should. Do I have a suggestion?"

Mark stood up. "I make a motion we vote Ben in as moderator."

"I second." Came from a voice somewhere in the back.

"Any opposed?" Jerry was glad he was almost through talking. He had written out what he was going to say last night and memorized it for just this occasion. "No. Alright, Ben come forward. I'll turn the show over to you."

Ben made his way to the pulpit and Jerry shook his hand on the way down. Ben stepped up to the microphone, his nervousness written on his face.

"Before we get started this morning, I think we should take a minute and bow our heads in prayer." Ben's deep voice helped set everyone's nerves at ease. He gave a brief but meaningful prayer. It wasn't pre-planned, it wasn't meant to impress it was straight from his heart. It was the voice of a concerned son talking to his wise and loving father.

"I guess at this time we'll have Pastor Knoll come forward and give his talk. Pastor." He held his arm out asking James to come forward.

As Pastor Knoll arrived at center stage he paused, with his head down, hands on either side of the pulpit. He raised his head slowly and looked out across the auditorium. He saw old friends, like Kramer and Bob, he saw new friends like Jack, he saw couples he had married and their kids he had baptized, he saw marriages nearly destroyed but through counseling now restored, he saw faces of people he had led to the Lord, teenagers that had surrendered for the ministry, and many eyes that had cried tears in his office or in his home, hands that had cooked him meals, people he had prayed for and prayed for him. He didn't see the lies and rumors that had been spread. He didn't see the hate in the eyes of some, he didn't see the guilt, or the vengeance.

"I appreciate all of you who came today." James sounded very subdued. Quiet but still commanding respect. He sounded like he was at peace with what he was going to say and in complete control. "Over the last few months a lot of things have happened. Some of you know what has been going on, some of you don't. I don't think we need to drag all of that out. I would however like to assure all of you that I would never and have never done anything to hurt any of you individually, or as a church. I know some of you got some misinformation about me, and if you have any questions, you should come to me personally. I have never made anything private, I have left my finances, and every decision I made open to any type of review or audit by any of you. I do think that as a whole, our church has done a poor job of being open in our communication with one another, with problems we have, or rumors we have heard. That is what destroys a church. If I could share with you for just a moment, turn in your Bibles to the fourth chapter of the book of James. We'll begin with verse 1. 'From whence come wars and fightings among you? Come they not hence, even of your lusts that war in your members? Ye lust, and have not: ye kill, and desire to have, and cannot obtain: ye fight and war yet ye have not. Ye ask, and receive not, because ye ask amiss, that ye may consume it upon your lusts.' Let's skip down to verse six. 'But.' This is the key. ' but, he giveth more grace. Wherefore he saith, God resisteth the proud, but giveth grace unto the humble. Submit yourselves therefore to God. Resist the devil, and he will flee from you. Draw nigh to God, and he will draw nigh to you. Cleanse your hands, ye sinners; and purify your hearts, ye double minded. Be afflicted, and mourn, and weep: let your laughter be turned to mourning, and your joy to heaviness. Humble yourself in the sight of the Lord, and he shall lift you up. Speak not evil one of another, brethren. He that speaketh evil of his brother, and judgeth his brother, speaketh evil of the law, and judgeth the law: but if thou judge the law, thou art not a doer of the law, but a judge. There is one lawgiver, who is able to save and destroy: who art thou that judgest another.' I believe that our church, not just our church but the global church as a whole, has failed. We have allowed peoples lives to be destroyed, souls turned away from salvation, and reputations to be shredded, in the name of unity. We gossip, and say 'so and so is so judgmental' when we are actually being the judge and jury for that person. We speak evil of one another and kill a ministry, or a growing new life, without even firing a shot. It's propaganda. I have spent the last thirty-six hours reevaluating my ministry here. God has shown me so much grace and allowed me to present Him and His Word to the community of Lendel for over fifteen years. I have loved, cared and shared, with all of you. I had to look at what has happened lately, honestly and objectively. I believe, with the damage done, God could more effectively use another man here to minister. Therefore, I am resigning as pastor of Lendel Community Church. I want all of you to know this is a decision my wife and I have made after much prayer, Godly counsel, and Bible study. We have no plan of where to go, but we know God will lead. This will be my last Sunday as your Pastor."

The auditorium was completely silent. No one moved. No one

made a sound. He had caught Jerry and Adam completely by surprise. Adam's plan of destroying him had been thwarted

All of a sudden, Alan Bennett stood to his feet. He excused his way out to the aisle and came forward to where Pastor Knoll was standing. He walked right up to him, threw his arms around his neck, and whispered something in his ear. James hugged him back. Right behind him was Jackson. Then Cassie, and one by one each of the youth came forward and hugged Pastor Knoll, telling him they loved him, or thanked him, or whatever it was they said. Even Gerry. Brad had never cried so hard in his life. James who had been fighting back the tears, let the dam break, and they rushed down his face.

Chapter 16

"Has your Dad decided where you guys are going to move to yet?"

Jason wondered why he had been called to the principal's office and was now getting his answer. "No, nothing certain yet."

"I still can't believe he resigned. I really thought he would stick it through to the bitter end. You know, it says an awful lot about your dad. It makes his faith seem real, and not just something he claims from the pulpit when everything is going good. I wish I could talk to him before he leaves."

"Why don't you?"

"Now? He's probably too busy figuring out what he needs to do."

"No. Just give him a call. He would love to hear from you."

"I don't think so Jason. We've had our differences in the past."

"Then this would be the best time to call him."

Principal Gibson didn't quite agree. "Well, I might. You can go ahead and go back to class now Jason. I was just wondering if your parents had decided to move, or stick around, or what?"

"Thanks Mr. Gibson." Jason closed the door behind him and let out a huge sigh of relief.

He hadn't done anything, but neither had his dad and look what had happened to him. He was scared when he heard his name called over the intercom, and thought about just leaving school. He knew he probably wouldn't be there much longer anyway.

His coach sure didn't want him to leave, he had even volunteered to let Jason live with them and finish out his Junior year as a Charger. Jason hadn't asked his parents yet but he was pretty sure they would say no. Besides Cassie, the only thing he would really miss was Basketball season. He thought they had a shot at taking State this year, and he had a chance to be All-State, maybe even first team. Now they might end up in some town that has a last place basketball team, or a team where because he's the new guy he might not get to play. These were all selfish reasons he knew, but he couldn't seem to get over them.

He got back to his chemistry class, and everyone started giving him the 'ooooo's' wondering why he had gone to the principal's office. Jason thought about telling them, but decided he would just let them wonder. He pulled out his chair and slid in behind the table, picking up where he and his lab partner left off.

The rest of the day went normal until right before his last class. Principal Gibson stopped him in the hall and asked him if his dad would be around this evening. Jason told him he thought so. They were going to the Y for about an hour when Jason got home but after that, he would be there. Principal Gibson thanked him, then hurried him off to class. Jason headed down the hall quite perplexed.

Mr. Gibson and his dad had been in disagreement since the first day Mr. Gibson took the job as principal. He had seemed anti-Christian, and since James was the most prominent pastor in the area, he had become an immediate target. James hadn't compromised anything in an attempt to be 'school friendly'. Some of the other pastors were used as counselors in school crisis situations, but they were not allowed to make any reference to God, or Jesus, or Christianity. They could refer to the generic 'a god' but that was as far as they could go. James' steadfastness on these issues was seen as a personal slap in the face to Mr. Gibson. Jason was amazed and excited about the interest Mr. Gibson was taking in his dad.

* * * *

Jerry stared at the door that had just slammed in his face. He wanted to kick it down and continue with the argument but he held back his anger for the moment. Rachael shoved her way by him, down the hall, and out the front door, without saying a word. Jerry wondered where she was headed, but his mind quickly came back to his situation at hand.

"Honey, please open the door." He waited a couple seconds. "Honey?" Still no answer. "Pam. I'm sorry."

The door opened a crack. "I'm not." There were tears streaming down Pam's face. "I don't even know who you are anymore Jerry."

"Pam, I told you that after all this stuff at the church is over I'll have more time for you guys. It's almost over."

"But Jerry, Oh I don't want to get into this again."

"Too late."

"Quit being such a jerk. Everything you say is so sarcastic. I'm sick of being around you Jerry. I think I need a break from you, or we need a break. Why don't we go away for awhile? We could go on a vacation for two weeks, or go camping or something."

"And where are we going to get the money for that?"

"You've made a ton with Adam. We could use some of that."

"I can't leave right now Pam, and I reinvested a lot of that money."

"I knew it. All you care about is money, and power. It scares me Jerry. I am begging you, please let's get away from all this for a while."

"We will. After we get another Pastor in here." The door slammed again. It felt like a slap in the face, only worse, because the person delivering it was out of sight. Jerry gave up pursuing the fight and turned to head towards the den. He plopped down in his recliner next to Gerry, who was watching T.V. As soon as he sat down, she got up and headed out of the room. Jerry didn't say anything, but it hurt him. His wife and him fought constantly, and his daughters wanted nothing to do with him. Not even for a short conversation. He was watching his family crumble. He just kept telling himself that it would all be back to normal soon.

He picked up the phone and dialed Adam's house. No answer. He wanted to talk to him and get some advice. He had asked Adam how Candy was taking all this, and apparently she was very supportive. That's exactly how he had imagined her to be. She was always supportive, always looking out for Adam and encouraging him. That's what Jerry wanted from Pam. He knew she was upset about what happened with the Pastor, but he wasn't the one who asked James to resign. James did that himself. In fact, they wanted the people to decide, they did all they could, James just decided to go. He couldn't understand why Pam blamed him. Soon she would see that this was best for the church anyway, especially when they have a new Pastor. In fact, they were having a meeting in two nights about a friend of Ben's that had expressed some interest.

I hope Bob doesn't show up. Bob had been very vocal the last three weeks, and had turned some of the church members sentiment against the deacons. He had even called for them to resign. He keeps saying 'this is our church' and trying to get people to oppose and question everything the deacons do. He had really been a thorn in Jerry's side ever since the Pastor resigned. His continuous babbling and argumentative spirit was hindering any progress to get past the situations and work on the future of the church. Jerry remembered their business meeting last Sunday when Bill had said that:

"The church is going to look for the man they deserve."

Bob stood up then and began one of his many speeches that day.

"That's what I'm afraid of. What kind of man do we deserve? The nation of Israel asked for a king, rejecting the plan God had already established, and God gave them the king they deserved. That's what I don't want, but I know we need. We need someone to come in here and tell us what we need to do, what we're doing right and what we're doing wrong. I think we should look for an older man that has a lot of experience, just as an interim for maybe a year, before we get started looking for a Pastor. We need a time to regroup, and get a focus of where God is leading us."

An interim. That was completely ridiculous. They needed to get a new Pastor in here right away and get over the past. People had quit tithing and they needed a Pastor to get them giving again. They needed a cause. Jerry was really worried about the financial situation they were in. They had already cut off all ties to the Institute, and three missionaries. They were barely able to make the building payment last month, and this month was going to be even tighter. He couldn't believe that Bob had wanted to give James a severance package, and even more unbelievable was that the church passed it. Luckily, James had turned it down. *So arrogant.*

"Jerry." Jerry jumped in his chair, surprised by Pam's voice behind him.

"What?" His voice was short, angry.

"I think I'm gonna go to my sister's tonight and come back on Friday. Geri and Rachel both said they want to go."

"I can't leave. I have that meeting."

"I know."

"What about school?" Jerry asked.

"They can miss a couple days."

"What about volleyball?"

"Jerry, their volleyball season ended two weeks ago." Pam was breathing hard to fight back the tears. *How could he not even know his daughter's volleyball season had ended?* "Anyway, my stuff is all packed, so I'll be back Friday. I'm gonna pick Rachael up at Cory's house."

Jerry almost asked who Cory was, but then remembered that Rachael had been dating him for about a month now.

"Well I guess I'll see you guys Friday then. Have fun."

"Yeah." Pam said heading out the front door with her travel bag.

Jerry heard the door open again and Pam call for Gerry. He heard her run down the stairs and out the door without even a bye. He shook his head and turned up the volume on the T.V.

* * * *

"Is she asleep?"

"I think so." Jenny said, tiptoeing out of Madeline's room, pulling the door closed part way.

"About time."

"What are you complaining about? I'm the one who has to get up with her in three hours."

"Well, I can't feed her."

Jenny laughed. Even though she was completely exhausted, Brad could still make her laugh. She pulled back their covers and got into bed.

"I am thoroughly worn out. My back hurts, my feet hurt, my legs hurt, my head hurts, every part of my body is painful."

"I'm sorry, honey. I feel bad for you. Is there anything I can do?"

"Yeah. Shut off the light and go to bed."

Brad turned off the light and rolled over in bed.

Bob ran his bath water as quietly as possible and slid into the tub almost silently. He was very adept at not waking up his wife, with all the crazy hours he worked. He started to immerse himself in the hot steamy water when he heard his wife whisper his name. Or maybe he was just dreaming. Then he heard it again.

"Bob. Is that you?"

He got out of the tub, wrapping the towel around his waist he poked his head out the door.

"Yes. I was in the tub."

Nancy was sitting up in their bed looking towards the hall. When she heard his voice, her head whipped around to him.

"No, I heard something downstairs."

"It was probably just me a few minutes ago." Bob glanced at the clock, which read 2:23. He had come in twenty minutes ago, so it was just her imagination he assured himself.

"No. It woke me up just a minute ago. Did you lock the door?"

"Yeah, I always do."

"Will you please go check?"

"Alright."

Bob headed down the stairs holding onto his towel tightly with his left hand. He felt a cool breeze as he reached the bottom of the stairs. The wind was giving him goose bumps, for two reasons. He turned left at the bottom of the stairs and saw the front door was open about four inches. He knew he had locked it. He always locked it. He felt someone move behind him and he whirled around, to see Jackson on the stairs right behind him.

"Jackson. You scared me to death." Neither of them was laughing like they normally would if one had scared the other.

"Sorry dad. I heard something a little bit ago and I came down here to see what it was."

Jackson's eye caught the open door also.

"Is someone in here?"

"I don't think so." Bob said and stepped outside to their front porch.

He stood there in his towel staring at the empty street in front of him. He was looking intently into the night, thinking the harder he looked, the easier it would be to see. He was staring so hard he almost didn't hear the laughing. It was soft at first. Eerie, but quiet. Bob turned to ask Jackson if he heard it, but he could tell by his face, he did. The laughing continued for about three minutes growing loud and close at times, then quiet and further away. It ended as quietly as it came.

"What do you think that was?" Jackson asked after staring into the dark for an uncomfortable amount of time.

"I have no idea."

The two men turned back into their house. They turned on all the lights and combed the entire structure, as if they were searching for a missing prisoner. They found nothing. Not even a hair. Finally, they went to bed. Jackson fell into a restless sleep about an hour later. Bob never did.

* * * *

Brad's eyes popped open. He looked over at the clock on the dresser. 2:21. He had been asleep for probably three hours. He was trying to figure out what had awakened him. He felt his arm hairs standing up on top of their goose bumps. He wasn't cold, but he had a disgusting feeling in the pit of his stomach.

"Are you awake honey?" Jenny's voice made him jump in bed.

"Yeah, are you?" *Stupid question.*

"Yeah. Did that noise wake you too?"

"I don't know. What noise?"

"That noise in the living room. Will you go check?"

Brad's goose bumps still hadn't gone down as he slid out of bed and pulled on a T-shirt. He slunk out of his room keeping near the wall in the shadows. Usually he was braver than this, heading out into the unknown, armed with only a baseball bat, but tonight his apprehension was set on high, and his weapon of choice was a five iron. He passed by Madeline's room pushing the door slightly and glancing in at the nursery. Everything was in order there. Next, he slid past the bathroom, his shadow falling across the toilet and tub. Empty. He stepped into the living room and felt the cold wind rush across his bare feet. He looked around to see if a window was open, but they were all closed. He followed the cool air to his front door. As he got right up to it, he noticed the door wasn't closed completely. He pushed it shut and then tried to reopen it. It was still locked. *How weird. I know it was shut when I locked it.* Just then, he heard it. The same as at camp, only further off. He opened the front door and stepped out on the lawn. The mumbling laughter was getting louder, it sounded like it wrapped his entire house, coming from all sides. The air seemed to drop ten degrees as the sounds closed in. Then all at once they quit. Brad stood there listening so intently, he thought his ears were going to bleed. Still nothing. He shook his head to make sure he wasn't dreaming and then heard the soft cry from Madeline. He saw the lights pop on to her room and he turned to head into the house. He was still listening for the laughter but could only hear the snow crunching under his bare feet. He stepped up the cement stairs that led into their house, his fear leaving him and the adrenaline that had been pumping was no longer there. He could now feel the cold burning his feet. Rushing in the house he plopped down, Indian style, right above a heat register holding his feet in the warm air rubbing them quickly with his hands. *Man, I wish we had a wood stove.* He could hear Jenny singing in the room next door. His feet finally warmed up a bit and he hurried to Madeline's room. He looked in to see Jenny facing him, with her finger across her lips. He nodded, backed out of the room and headed for bed. She came to bed a few minutes later.

"Did you hear all that?" Jenny surprised Brad with her question. He didn't think she would be able to hear it in the house.

"Yeah. Kinda creepy huh?"

"Kinda? It was really creepy. Who was doing that?"

"I don't think it was a who. Remember at camp? Well it was the same thing."

"No wonder you were so freaked out."

"Yeah. Do you think you'll be able to fall asleep?"

"No."

"Me either. Do you mind if I read the Bible for a while?"

"No. Please do."

Chapter 17

Bill read the message over again.

Bill,

I need to talk to you about some work you had done in the rail mill. We are having a meeting at 9:30 about the accident last night, but I need to see you before that.

Dan

All types of images and fears were running through Bill's mind. He wished he could take back all the payments he had authorized, but there was no way. He kept thinking he was going to throw up, but every time he rushed to the bathroom, nothing came up. He thought about just quitting, just walking out the door and never coming back, except that if there was just a chance he could get out of this, it was worth it. He made decent money, the benefits were great, and if he walked out, he would have a hard time getting a job anywhere. He would have to come up with some kind of a lie. Maybe they would only be investigating this one job, because of the accident last night. Maybe he could just blame Lendel Manufacturing. They didn't complete the job they were hired for, or maybe they did complete it, but it was just faulty. He was trying to remember what work had been authorized in the rail mill, but he couldn't come up with it. He had shredded all the receipts, except for the ones he had to staple to the Payment for Work Completed documents. He glanced over at the clock. It was 8:15. *I wonder what time Dan expects me.* He got his answer just then.

He answered the ringing phone and Dan asked him to come to his office then. Bill tried to sound upbeat and confident on the phone, but felt beat and apprehensive as he headed down the hall. He tapped lightly on the door and heard Dan's voice from inside.

"Door's open."

Bill stepped inside. "Morning Dan."

"Morning. You hear what happened last night?"

"Some. I know there was an accident in the rail mill. I don't know where or what, or how bad."

"It was at the #2 Intermediate. Apparently they were just finishing up with a roll change and were sending the first bar through to tighten everything up, when one of the two inch casters, broke on the Fly wheel and the rail came up over the top, taking out both men up on the cap. One just got banged up pretty bad, the other, a guy named Jim Ochs, had the rail knock him off then land on top of him. He burned to death before they could cut the rail off him."

Bill's face was white. Bob would have been there last night, and he probably was trying to cut the rail off Jim. He could just picture him screaming while the men were trying to get it off him.

"The entire Rail Mill is going to be shut down for a week. You can still smell burnt flesh in there, and all the guys that night are pretty shook up. But the reason I called you in here is, the caster that broke, you authorized payment on one three days before."

"So it was faulty?" Bill felt relieved.

"No. That's what we thought at first. We contacted Bob Grant, the Maintenance Foreman in the Rail Mill--"

"--yeah I know him--"

"--and he said they never got a new caster. The caster that was on there was about six years old. The life on those things is five years. He said he had submitted requests several times but they had been shot down as 'not essential'. So, what's going on."

Bill was trying to figure something out in his mind. What could he say to get out of this one.

"Maybe Bob got one and didn't know it. Or maybe they weren't quite finished with the new one, I don't know. It's not my job to follow up on everyone, I just pay the bills."

"I know Bill, I'm not blaming you, I just think you should know, when we go into that meeting today they are going to be looking for a scapegoat, and you better be ready. Hey, before you leave, did you make any other payments to Lendel Distributing. They're gonna want to know, and see if they can pin something on them."

"I might have. I can't remember every bill, Dan."

"Alright. See you at 9:30."

"See you."

Bill sat down in his office chair. He looked at the clock again. It was already 9:05. He cursed under his breath. What was he going to tell his wife. He would most likely get fired if they had any type of investigation. Unless he could cover his tracks better. He opened the phone book and turned to the L's. He had never thought he would need a lawyer, but he was looking for one now. He looked over at the clock. It was 9:20. *I guess I better go down stairs.* He walked down the stairs, through the long hall, and turned into the meeting room. He closed the door behind him. The hall sat empty for two hours until the door finally came open again, and Bill was the first to exit. He headed out the front doors, shielding his eyes from the reflection off the snow, jumped in his truck and headed off without giving it a chance to warm up first.

As he came up to Sycamore Lane, he thought about just passing it by. He didn't. He pulled into his house and trudged up the slick sidewalk. He stomped his feet to rid them of the snow and stepped inside. Dorothy was sitting on the couch reading a book, and was surprised by her husband's early entrance.

"Honey, I'm glad you're home." She jumped off the couch and gave him a big hug. "How did you get off so early?"

"It's a long story." He began rubbing the back of his neck. "I am suspended from work indefinitely."

"Suspended? Why?"

"There was an accident in the Mill last night, and I guess they needed someone to blame."

"That's not fair. You weren't even there last night." "I know. I don't really know what's going on."

"Come here." Dorothy held her arms out and Bill gave her a big hug.

He hadn't told her, they had already checked his other payments, that had never been completed, that they had talked with Lendel Manufacturing, who didn't even know they had received any payment, and that he was not only under investigation for embezzlement, but also for negligence, and reckless endangerment. He was also told Jim's family might try to get a manslaughter charge brought against him.

* * * *

James was helping Hannah clear their coffee table. Jack and Janice had left about ten minutes ago. James still couldn't believe the change in Jack's attitude toward him in the last month or so. He had just mentioned they were going to rent a trailer to take some stuff up to Robert in Denver.

"No. You can just take my truck and trailer." Jack had said.

"I can't do that. You might need it."

"Don't argue with a dying man." Jack laughed at his own joke. "I might want to tag along. If that'd be alright."

"Sure. I really appreciate it Jack."

They had come over for dinner, and stayed for coffee afterward. James heard a lot of stories about Lendel and the church he had never heard before. Apparently Hank Peters wife, Susan, died when Bill was just eight. She was in a car accident. Kramer Binx parents owned both banks at one time. When they passed away, Kramer sold them to two different corporations and donated most of the money to the school, church and town. He was only 18 years old when this happened. Jack's parents had been homesteaders in Lendel. It was one of the few places in Colorado that you could still rope off an area and claim it as yours. Jack could remember when they would wait for the train to bring in mail and other supplies that they had needed. Even though Lendel usually had a mild climate, they were really cut off from the rest of Colorado. They sat so low in the valley, during winter months it was almost impossible to get through some of the passes. Bridgeline Pass was usually closed from November through March. James and Hannah listened to the Johnson's stories and even shared a few of their own. Around 9:00, Jack figured they better head home. He was having trouble seeing at night, and the snow was starting to come down a little heavier, so they said their good byes and left.

"I wish we could have gotten to know them better." Hannah said wistfully.

"Me too. At least God gave us the chance to know a little bit about them, and have an opportunity to share in some of their past."

"Yeah. I never imagined that. I didn't think we would ever be having dinner with Jack and Janice, and not be arguing."

"Me either."

The phone rang and interrupted their conversation. Hannah got to it first.

"Hello…Oh hi. Sure, just a minute." Hannah covered the phone with her hand. "It's Principal Gibson."

James looked puzzled. *Frank Gibson? Oh man, Jace.* He reached for the phone and Hannah handed it to him.

"This is James."

"Uh, hi James. This is Frank Gibson. Sorry to be bothering you so late, but uh Jason said it would be alright if I called. I was wondering, could we get together sometime and talk. I have some questions I need to ask you."

"Sure. When would be a good time for you?"

"How about in twenty minutes."

"Twenty minutes?"

"If that's okay."

"Yeah. Do you want me to come over there or…"

"Can we just meet at Betty's Diner?"

"That's fine. So I'll see you in twenty minutes then."

"James."

"Yeah."

"Thanks." With that, Principal Gibson hung up.

"What was that all about?" Asked Hannah.

"I don't know exactly. Apparently, Frank wants me to meet him at Betty's diner in twenty minutes. He said he has some questions for me. Man, I hope Jace didn't do something stupid."

"Maybe you should call him. I think he's over at Cassie's."

"Good idea."

James quickly called over to Cassie's house and asked Jason

about it. Jason explained his meeting with the principal and assured James he had done nothing wrong. James believed him and felt relieved.

As he pulled up to Betty's, James could already see Frank sitting in a booth near the back. Frank usually looked so in charge, so in command, but tonight he looked nervous. James watched as Frank put one finger after another to his mouth, biting quickly on his nails. After he finished chewing them as far as the pain would allow he began popping his knuckles. James decided to go in and talk with him.

When he got to the booth, Frank stood up and shook his hand. He had waved him over as soon as James stepped in the front door.

"Thanks for coming James."

"No problem."

The waitress stopped by and James ordered a piece of pie and some ice cold milk. Frank passed.

"I don't know exactly where to start. Why'd you do it?"

"Resign?"

Frank nodded his head.

"Well…one reason was because I didn't want to send the church into a vote and end up splitting. Whether we like it or not, the entire community recognizes Lendel Community Church as a growing, alive church. To some, and I hesitate to say this, but it is the representation of Christians in whole, and when they see problems like this going on, it just tarnishes or even refutes all the ministering or testimony we have tried to provide this community. I wanted this church to get back to a place of respectability within the community. A second reason is because of the size of Lendel. Everyone saw my picture in the paper, and read the caption underneath. I have not had one single person come to me individually and ask what it was all about. That tells me people either believed it or didn't. If they believed it, all the credibility I have gained over the last fifteen years was destroyed in one day, and I might not ever get it back. The things some of the members of our church have said about me, I might not ever get back to where people can trust me. And the last reason… I think God was saying 'It's time to move on'."

"Wow. But didn't part of you just want to stick it out? Fight it out? Lash out?"

"Sure. Sometimes I wanted to sue the paper, attack some of the men in our church from the pulpit, and at least have a chance to defend myself. Then I read this verse and it talked about counting it joy when people falsely accuse you, and say evil about you. I thought 'that doesn't make any sense.' Then I began thinking about Jesus, and what he went through. He was falsely accused, people lied about him, beat him, spit on him, mocked him, and finally murdered him. He didn't complain. He didn't say poor me. He watched the hands he had made, pound violently against his face, he saw the lips he had made, curse him, lie about him, spit on him. He saw the people he had given life to try to take his, and you know what he did? He said "Father, forgive them, for they know not what they do." He forgave them, and then begged God to do the same, he was even willing to take their punishment for the way they treated him. He died because of them, just as he died because of me and you, but then offered us eternal life if we would just accept it. He suffered the ultimate price, so how could I justify me being upset about a few lies and maybe having to move. I'm still alive."

"You really believe all that stuff don't you."

"Sure I do--"

"--I never did." Frank interrupted before James could continue. "I always thought that it was just a crutch people used, or a way to earn respect, or a social deal. I always thought that, until lately. You know how we have gotten along in the past, and part of that was the fact that you completely destroyed my opinion of Christians. You lived it, and the people in your church lived it. When you said you cared for someone, you really cared for someone. Your love wasn't just a dutiful love, it was genuine love that you don't see very often. I guess that's the biggest thing. Nothing seems dutiful to you, it all seems natural. When all the things started happening a few months ago, I didn't believe what I heard, but I found myself wanting them to be true. I think that's where most people were. They knew they weren't, but in a way, they wanted them to be. I kept waiting for you to lose your cool, to go on the offensive, and you never did. Your life made Christianity real. I want to be real. I want the love and compassion you have for people. I want the contentment you have. I want to know Jesus like you know him. I want him to be as real to me as he is to you."

James didn't even notice his tears until one fell on his hand. He was staring at Frank who was looking down now. If all the things that had happened, were for this moment, it was worth it. James was taken aback at what he had said, but the Holy Spirit prompted him and gave him the words to say. James and Frank bowed their heads there in Betty's Diner, and Frank prayed to God for salvation.

They talked for a little while after that, both very excited, and James agreed to disciple him until he left for a church somewhere. They also agreed to have Bob come to their Bible studies to pick up wherever James and him would leave off when James left. James finally got up to leave but Frank wanted to stay by himself for a while. He was deciding how he was going to swallow his pride and tell his wife. He was excited, and nervous at the same time. James said he would go along with him, but Frank said no. As James headed to his car, he glanced back and saw Frank actually kneeling at his booth in prayer.

"Thank you, Lord." James whispered. "Thank you."

Chapter 18

Jerry dialed the number again. He tried one more time before he left for the meeting that night. He heard it ring the third time, fourth, and finally the fifth. He slammed the phone down. He had been trying to call Pam for two days now, and had gotten no answer. Not even a "they're not here right now." *Great. I don't need all this on my mind tonight too.* Jerry shrugged it off and headed out the door. *Priorities*, he kept telling himself. He talked himself into the fact that he was doing the right thing. He had thought about driving up to his sister-in-law's but decided this meeting was too important. After this, then they would be able to work things out. He'd have more time. Anyway, he was the speaker. He had to be there. He was in charge.

It didn't take him long to get to the church. No one was there when he arrived, and he was glad. He wanted a few more minutes to spend alone, give himself time to think. This was the third meeting he had run. After Pastor Knoll resigned, he had been in charge of setting up meetings, and overseeing the course that their meetings took. He unlocked the front door, then Pastor Knoll's old office. Jerry had adopted it for his own. He opened the right hand desk drawer and pulled out a pad of paper. He took the pen off the top of the desk, and began jotting down some of the topics he thought they needed to touch on tonight, including Ben's friend. Jerry filled about a page and a half, before he decided to start deleting some topics. He was completely engrossed with his project, not seeing Brad come in, standing in the doorway.

"You left your lights on."

Jerry jumped. "My lights?"

"Yeah, on your car. You left them on.""Uh, thanks." Jerry kept scribbling on the paper.

"I would have shut them off but your car was locked."

"Alright Brad I'll get to it!"

Brad shook his head and walked away. He had just been trying to help. Even after all this time, Jerry still couldn't talk civilly to him. Brad had made every attempt to restore at least some semblance of the relationship they had had before, but Jerry wanted no part of it.

Brad headed to the sanctuary, where they were going to have the meeting tonight. He stepped in and looked around. It saddened him to see the auditorium completely empty. The past two Sundays, there had almost been as few people in there for the morning service as there was now. Their attendance had decreased nearly 40% while their youth had remained the same. Brad was expecting about 150-200 people tonight for the meeting. He was praying Jerry wouldn't say something too dumb and turn off even more members. He knew they were going to bring up Ben's friend, for them to vote on for a chance to candidate. In a way he thought they should probably let him come, he had listened to both sides on the issue and they both had good points. He agreed with Bob that they needed an older interim, until they got some things right as a church body, but he also agreed with Adam that they needed to get someone in right away to stop the bleeding. He was looking forward to some debating on this subject tonight, as long as it didn't get out of hand.

Something else was bothering Brad. They hadn't even begun discussing a pulpit committee. He was worried that the deacons were just going to avoid the issue as long as they could so they would be able to have control as long as possible. This was not only bothering Brad, but several of the older members had mentioned being concerned as well. This was probably the biggest decision Lendel Community Church had been faced with in years, and they wanted to make sure they were following God's plan as best they could. However, some people didn't even want to discuss anything about a new Pastor. They were still bitter over Pastor Knoll leaving, and blamed the deacons, and even to some extent Brad, for letting him leave. They were still trying to think of ways to get James to come back and wanted no part of finding his replacement.

It wasn't long before people began filing into the church. Jerry had set some chairs up on the stage, where he, Adam, Bill, and Jack would sit. Brad noticed some people shaking their heads as they came in seeing the chairs up there. They must have thought it as egotistical as Brad did.

"Hi honey." Brad turned around to see Jenny right behind him. She had gotten a ride to the doctors with Hannah, who apparently had dropped her off here tonight. Brad was glad. Jenny had missed most of their meetings, so Brad was glad she was going to get in on this one. He had been trying to relay information to her, but a lot of the time he had mangled it.

Brad gave her a hug. "Good to see you. How's our little girl?" He said kissing Madeline on the cheek.

"She's fine. The doctor said she's very alert for being 1 month old. She watched him everywhere he moved. I think she thought he was you."

Brad laughed. "Must be the hair."

Jenny smiled with him. "I think I'm gonna stay with her in the nursery tonight and listen over the speaker. We're not gonna have to vote on anything are we?"

"We shouldn't, but with Jerry at the helm you never know what to expect."

Jenny gave him a small peck on the lips, and shouldering her diaper bag, headed for the nursery. Brad turned down the aisle and took a seat neat the front.

Before long, Adam and Candy came in. Candy came over and sat right next to Brad. He felt a little uncomfortable. Candy had always made him feel uncomfortable, she always sat too close, or hugged too long, or was too touchy, for Brads liking. Even Jenny had noticed it, and warned him about her. Brad didn't even like talking to her, and avoided her most Sundays, but here she was, sitting right next to him. Adam headed up on stage and took his seat. He was followed quickly by Jerry, Bill, and then much later a hesitant Jack.

It seemed more like Adam was the speaker than Jerry. It seemed like he was the sports Icon, or movie star, or Rock star, and the deacons were his entourage. Sometimes it completely disgusted Brad. He decided to look around and see who had come in, attempting to avoid talking to Candy. Maybe he could make it look like he was waiting for someone, and then he could move without being to obvious.

As his eyes shifted quickly, trying not to strain his neck too much, he noticed Bob, and Mark, he noticed Phillip, Kramer, and Ben. Just as noticeable by their absence, were Pam and her two daughters, plus every single member of his youth department. That worried Brad a little. He had figured most of them would have shown since they were just as interested, if not more, than 90% of the people here. What Brad didn't know is that the letter sent out, announcing to everyone the meeting for tonight, included a statement that no one under twenty would be allowed this evening. 'Do to the seriousness of matters at hand, and to prevent any type of disturbance we request only those twenty and above attend the meeting.' Brad had not been given this letter. It had been mailed out two days prior.

Besides the youth, where was Pam? *Maybe they are coming in two cars.* Brad kept saying, but he didn't believe it. Something was telling him they were having trouble on the home front, which could spell trouble for the meeting tonight.

* * * *

Alan was standing in front of the group gathered at Bob Grant's house. Jackson had volunteered his parent's house for the Youth group to use tonight for their prayer meeting and Bible study. Alan was nervous as he asked them to open their Bibles. He was now the unspoken commander of the youth group. No one would ever say it to another person, but inside they all admired Alan. He had become a hero, a spiritual leader, and it was obvious to all. All that is, except Alan. He was still the shy, almost to where it hurt, quiet kid he always was, away from church or the youth group, but once these kids got together, he changed completely. He allowed the walls to come down, the walls that had been built over time, through years and years of being the butt of jokes, being the last kid picked at every sport, having to wear not only braces but also head gear, glasses, corrective shoes, and a retainer. But inside the youth group, he was seen as an equal, what was preached was practiced. "For God is no respecter of persons." The same was true here. Even lately at school, Alan was starting to open up, especially since all the kids carried their admiration for him over into their daily lives, and the group began hanging out more as a group. Not just on Sundays and youth nights, but they even met once a day at their school, during lunch to pray.

As Alan began speaking, the kids all listened. They had heard the story of Jonah many times before, but this evening, Alan was relating it to their lives. To their lives at exactly this time. The longer he spoke the more comfortable he became, and the more he made the story come alive to the rest of the kids. After he finished speaking, there was a brief discussion and then they broke into small groups to pray. Mostly they prayed for the decisions that would be made this evening, but there was some time spent in prayer for their Principal.

Jason had told them about Principal Gibson getting saved, and the kids had already seen some changes in him at school. It had only been two days, but he seemed more sincere, more concerned about them than he had in the past. It was such an encouragement seeing him get saved, and also gave them a boost to witness, thinking if he could get saved, anyone could.

Cassie closed the group in prayer, but none of the kids left. They all stayed around, worrying about the meeting tonight. A couple kids suggested that they might be trying to get rid of Brad and that's why they weren't allowed to be there.

* * * *

"I still don't feel right about this." It was Phillip expressing his concern, rather than Bob this time.

"Phillip." Adam took the floor now. He had remained quiet until this point. "We know that there is going to be some differing viewpoints on the matter of calling a Pastor. If we wait until everyone is in agreement, we may never end up even getting one to candidate. Just because we are asking a man to come and preach a

Sunday doesn't mean we have to hire him. It is just getting us exposed to different men so we can make an informed decision. Maybe we will decide to call an interim like you and Bob want, or maybe we will hire a pastor, only God knows. But we can't limit Him by not allowing someone to speak just because it's not what we want."

Brad felt Candy nod her head in agreement. He hated that it was just him and her in the whole pew, and she was sitting so close to him he could feel her breathing. He had moved all the way to the edge and each time she had scooted, all be it slyly, closer to him. They weren't touching, but very close. It also seemed to Brad that Jerry was giving him dirty looks. Almost like he was her husband and not Adam.

There was a brief pause then Adam continued. "We appreciate all the time everyone has spent, in prayer or conversation, on the matter before us. We feel like this has been good for us to express our concerns. I want you to know, we have already considered all these, and they have been brought up at our meetings. We have not taken lightly the responsibility you have given to us and we covet your prayers."

Brad couldn't believe what he was hearing. *What responsibility? We haven't asked or approved anything for you guys.* He was looking around expecting to see Bob stand up, but he didn't. He felt like he should, but then didn't. He had withdrawn himself a lot from the church business, and completely focused on the youth and youth matters. He no longer was concerned with the church and the stupid decisions it made. In a way, it was sad but it was the only way to keep from getting so angry he did something stupid.

Adam continued on, becoming more eloquent, and more deceitful with every line. Brad looked around and everyone seemed completely mesmerized with his every word. It disgusted Brad. He had never been able to see how the Anti-Christ could blind so many people, but now seeing a mere man do it to an entire church, he could see it happening. Mercifully, Adam ended. Brad was happy and ready to go home. Adam asked Brad to dismiss them in prayer, and let everyone know they could pick up a vote card on the back table on their way out. They had to have it back in by Sunday. Brad stood to pray but was interrupted before he could even start.

"I wasn't going to say anything tonight. I am as tired with all the arguing and bickering as anyone else, but I felt compelled too." Bob's deep voice had a way of making your bones rattle, and whether you wanted to listen to him or not, you always did. "I heard all that Adam said, and it sounded good. Except for the fact that we haven't asked him to do anything for our church. He's not a deacon, he's not a trustee, he holds no office nor been appointed to one. We have sat back and allowed him to act like he runs the show. Aren't you the Speaker Jerry?" The sarcasm in his question was plain to all. "Before we do anything, we need to elect a pulpit committee, who will govern and make decisions concerning a Pastor or interim for this church. We cannot allow these four men to make every decision. Only three of them are deacons. We need a new election. Or at least another deacon."

Adam stood up again. He walked slowly to the center of the stage, a few feet back from the pulpit. He put his right hand up to his face and moved his fingers up and down his jaw line keeping his thumb on the opposite side. After a few seconds he paused, then spoke quietly.

"We have talked extensively about this very thing. If we wanted a change in leadership, then we need a change in all the leadership. Not just the pastor. We have talked about resigning, but agreed it would be best for the church, that we wait until we have a Pastor and he gets settled in. We are the only ones who have been deeply involved with decision making of the church the last couple years, and it would be very hard for new men to step in right away." He looked back at the deacons and they all shook their heads in agreement. All except Jack.

"What do you mean by we?" Jack asked Adam.

"Well you, that's what I mean. Before Pastor Knoll left, I had been invited to several deacons meetings, and was able to express my opinion. I'm only up here because I am concerned about the future of this church. I want to do what is best for this church. That's all."

"Well I also have one brief thing to say." Jack didn't stand but remained seated while he talked. "Most of you know I have been diagnosed with cancer. It's very advanced and I probably won't live to see the New Year. I have a lot of regrets in my life. One is that I never gave Pastor Knoll a chance. I would like to apologize to you, as I have to him, for always causing problems, and being more than the devil's advocate. But to his credit, he still did so much in spite of me. I want you all to know, if there was anyway to get James back I'd do it. But there's not. I might not live to see another Pastor in here, but I do think we should elect someone to take my place. This is too big a job for just Jerry and Bill, and it's getting to be too much for me to handle. I know this is short notice but I think we should consider Ben as a replacement. We could give him a trial run for the next ninety days and see how it goes. That is if he would be willing to accept. We need another old goat, to take the place of this old goat."

There was some light chuckle through the audience, while everyone was turning to look at Ben. He nodded his head. Adam stepped up to the microphone.

"Should we take a vote? All in favor raise your right hand...Any opposed? Alright Ben we'd like to welcome you as one of the Lendel Community deacons." Adam winked at Candy but nobody seemed to notice. Just yesterday, he and Ben had signed a contract on a cleaning business they had bought together. It had gone up for sale two days before, and Adam worked out the details with Ben, allowing him to be a silent partner, just investing. They had taken possession of the lucrative company yesterday, and Adam had promised a sizable dividend by the end of November.

Chapter 19

"So you're going in two weeks, huh?" Frank was happy for James, but at the same time was sad that he might be losing his teacher.

"Yeah, they want us to come and candidate two weeks from this Sunday."

"Are you excited?"

"Sure. I love the ocean and I've always wanted to live on the east coast, plus I hear the Carolinas are absolutely beautiful."

"They are. How did you hear of this church?"

"A friend of mine from college told me about it. He wanted to know if I had any students from the Institute who might be interested. I told him I'd find out. Hannah and I talked to one couple but they didn't really want to move that far from home. I called my buddy back last week to see if they had called someone yet, and they hadn't. So I sent them my resume, and then they asked me to come preach."

"How big a church is it?"

"I guess around 150. It's in a pretty small town, only about 10,000. We got on the internet last night and looked it up. They finished second in state at basketball last year and that got Jace pretty excited."

"I'll bet." Agreed Frank. "That's been his major concern this whole time, I think."

"Well that, and Cassie."

"Oh yeah. That's gonna be pretty hard on him I bet."

"Yeah, but he thinks they are going to go to the same college, and with e-mail and all that they can keep in touch pretty good. Plus he's young."

"Not to change the subject, but I have some questions about the Old Testament."

Frank and James had a good discussion on some of the laws and traditions of the Old Testament and even the importance of it in today's society. James was amazed at how much Frank had learned in such a short time. His questions were very deep and insightful, they weren't easily answered, and more than once James had to say, "I'll get back to you with an answer." Frank's growth had really encouraged him and Bob. However, Bob was a little nervous about taking over the discipleship of Frank. He said he felt inadequate, but James explained to him how all of us are inadequate, but with the Holy Spirit's help, we can make the Bible come to life for men like Frank.

"Well I was kind of waiting for Bob to show up before I told you, but it doesn't look like he's going to make it." He paused trying to build the drama. "You remember how I told you about that night after you left Peggy's Diner and I went home and told Debra I had received Jesus Christ as my personal Savior, and at first she laughed. Well this afternoon, she asked if I could explain to her exactly what that meant. I did and I even asked her if she wanted to pray with me. She declined. Tonight though when I was leaving to come over here, she asked if I thought you would mind if she dropped by after her kitchenware show she was going to. I told her I didn't think you would mind."

"No not at all."

"James, I really think she is going to get saved tonight. I've been praying for her every single hour since I got saved. Literally, God has woke me up, every hour on the hour, and I have prayed for her salvation. Do you think Hannah would be willing to talk to her?"

"I'm sure she would be. But Frank, don't get discouraged if she doesn't get saved tonight. It will probably take some time, and you want it to be genuine, not just a profession of faith. Jesus said you must confess with your mouth AND believe in your heart. Her belief will come by seeing you, your changed life. You don't want her to make a snap decision just so she doesn't feel like she is missing out on a part of your life, but that she truly believes."

"Yeah, I know. But I still hope tonight is the night."

Both men laughed. They spent some more time talking, just about life in general, the difficulties of being a high school principal, and the even harder job of being a Christian principal. They talked about their kids, James even talked some about his grand kids. They talked about the Chargers chances at basketball now that they were most likely going to lose Jace and also where they thought Jackson would go to play football.

Finally, Debra showed up. There were some formal introductions, since all the parties knew who each other were, they just didn't know each other. They chatted again for what seemed like only an hour but when they heard the Grandfather clock in the living room it struck twelve.

"Wow, is that clock correct?" Frank asked surprised.

James looked at his watch. "Yeah. 12:00 exactly."

"We better get going honey I've got school tomorrow."

Frank and Debra stood up to leave and the Knoll's walked them to the door. They stood there until they had got into their cars and headed for home.

"I really like Debra." Hannah said.

"You sound like you're surprised that you do."

"I am. She had always seemed so snotty at ball games, and activities."

"That's how I used to feel about Frank. Between them and the Johnson's, it's making it awfully hard to leave this area."

"Yeah, I know. It's been a long time since we've had friends our age, with the same interests as us. You know, with more in common than just the church."

"I know exactly what you mean." James said in agreement.

* * * *

Bob heard the thud and then the plop, plop, plop sound of his shredded tire slapping the pavement. He turned on his hazards and pulled off the highway and onto the shoulder. His wife stayed in the car while he jumped out to check the tire. He went around to the back of the truck to see which one blew. But it wasn't one. It was both. He had just bought these tires a week ago, and they had both blown. That seemed more than just a coincidence to Bob. Immediately jumping to the front of his mind was Jerry. He could see him doing something like that. Putting some kind of a pin hole in them, to compromise the integrity of the tire wall, or even somehow plant nails on the road. Then the reality hit him. If Jerry was actually going to do something, he would have slashed them. He wouldn't have been able to plan a blowout, let alone a double blowout. Just then, Bob felt someone behind him. It felt like they were reaching for his neck, so he spun around quickly. There was no one there. He felt spooked. He rubbed his hands together to warm them up a bit. He looked down at the tires one more time. *That's just too weird. Both of them.* He felt someone behind him again, so he headed for the cab. He wanted to run, but felt to silly running from nothing. He looked over his shoulder again as he reached the truck door. Nothing. He jumped in the cab and slammed the door. He felt the whole cab shake from the heavy metal door.

"What happened?"

"Both back tires blew."

"Both of them?" Nancy asked curiously.

"Yep. Can you believe it? Both of them." Bob was shaking his head.

"So what are we gonna do now?"

"I guess we'll call a tow truck, and then I'll call James and tell him I'm gonna be late for the Discipleship course tonight."

Nancy handed him the cell phone from inside her purse. Bob turned it on to dial information, but got the annoying 'no service' message.

"No service, we're only three miles from town. How can we have no service?" Nancy didn't answer since it looked like Bob was talking to the phone.

"So what are we going to do now?" Nancy asked getting a little worried. The truck was starting to get cold, and she was still in her dress, from their date earlier this evening.

"I guess walk."

"In high heels? I don't think so. Can't you just get to the top of that hill? The signal should reach from there."

Bob said okay and left his wife his coat. He put on a stocking cap and headed up the hill. He reached the top, and got the 'no service' message once again. He headed down the hill to the truck completely frustrated. He was about thirty yards away from the truck when he felt like someone was following him again. He hurried to the truck and jumped in the semi-warm cab.

"Well?" Nancy was looking at him expectantly.

"No service. Have you noticed not one single car has passed by us in the last thirty or so minutes we've been sitting here."

"They must have closed the roads to the Springs."

"Yeah but still, you'd think at least one car would have come by." Bob was getting worried. Something wasn't right about all this. He didn't want to worry Nancy but he knew they needed to keep moving and find some shelter and a phone pretty quick. "Honey, I'm sorry, but I really think we need to start walking towards town. I don't know why our phone isn't working, and no one has passed by, we need to get going. The truck's not going to get any warmer."

"Can't we run the engine and turn on the heat?"

"No. Carbon monoxide. You ready?" Bob opened his door and headed around to hers. She had it open and he carried her out of the snowy ditch, setting her down on the pavement. He locked the doors with his remote and they headed in the direction of Lendel. Faces pointed downward, head first into the blowing snow.

* * * *

It was Saturday and Jerry was getting worried. He tried calling his sister-in-laws again. No answer. *They have caller I.D.* He flipped the T.V. on and immediately the phone rang.

"Hello."

"Hi Jerry, this is Candy."

"Hi Candy. How are you?"

"Fine. I was just calling to ask you, well Adam's going out of town tonight for business, and I was wandering if you and Pam would like to come over for dinner?"

Jerry couldn't believe his ears. "Well Candy, Pam's not here either. She's at her sister's."

"That's right. You told me that the other day."

Jerry knew she had remembered that, she was just playing it off like she didn't know so it didn't sound bad. "I don't have anything to do tonight, so I could come over if you'd like."

"Uh, sure, I guess. About 6:30."

"Sounds great. See you then."

Chapter 20

Jerry looked at the case sitting on the seat next to him. He pulled up to a light and opened it up again. He looked at the shiny silver barrel reflecting off the dark black handle. He had always wanted a pistol. He had two rifles at home he used for hunting, but this pistol was different. It had felt so comfortable in his hand, and the guy at the pawn shop said he looked like a natural. He couldn't wait to take it out to the gun range and fire off a few rounds. He had purchased both regular and hollow point bullets, for his new .357 Magnum pistol. The first time he had noticed this particular model he was looking at a magazine. He fell in love with it immediately and was blown away when he saw it in the pawn shop. It was a lot heavier than he thought it would be. He picked it up again and bounced it off his leg. The light turned green and he accelerated through the light. Just moving his finger around the trigger guard gave him a sense of power. He felt almost invincible, like no one could mess with him. He felt a little taller, a little younger, a little stronger, all because of the hard plastic butt in his hand.

He had needed a confidence boost. His ego had taken quite a hit over the last few months. It seemed like only yesterday he had been invited over to Candy's for dinner. Just him and Candy. He had gotten ready quickly and headed on over. Candy already had the table set and dinner ready when he got there. They finished dinner and had a nice dessert. He waited around while she put the kids to bed, and then they moved to the living room to talk. Everything was going exactly like he had imagined. She set the coffee down on the coffee table and he moved over to the couch next to her. She had seemed nervous and kept adjusting herself on the couch, pulling on the bottom of her skirt each time she moved. Jerry was nervous too, but he had gone over this so many times in his mind, it seemed only like a dress rehearsal. He moved a little closer on the couch, and she continued to talk about the church. He wished she would stop, but he decided she was just trying to settle her nerves.

"Would you like a cup of coffee, Jerry?" Jerry nodded his head as she reached forward to grab the coffeepot.

This was his chance, he had to make his move now. As she leaned forward, Jerry bent down and kissed her. She pulled away quickly, completely in shock.

"What are you doing?" Candy yelled at him wiping her mouth.

"I-I-I'm sorry. I thought, well you know." Jerry looked down. "Sorry." He got up and hurried out, not even saying bye. He had never been so humiliated in his whole life. He honestly wanted to die. He thought about just driving off Skyline Drive, but talked himself out of it. He was really feeling bad, and worried about what Adam would do when he found out. *Should I call her and ask her not to tell him. No that would just make it seem worse.* He finally pulled up to his house and saw his wife's car in the drive. *Finally something good.* But he was over confident. He came inside and Pam was standing there waiting for him.

"Honey, I'm glad your home." Jerry said moving toward Pam to give her a hug. She stepped away.

"Where were you tonight?" She asked.

Where was I? She was the one that's been gone for so long. "I went to get something to eat." *What's it to you.*

"Where?"

"Just a drive-thru. Why?"

Tears were filling Pam's eyes. She turned and headed down the hall. Her voice trailing off. "You have some messages."

Jerry was staring at her as she headed down the hall. He picked up the phone and punched in his voice mail code.

"Hi Jerry, this is Candy. You're probably not home yet, but I just wanted to let you know, I won't tell Adam about your kiss. He thinks so highly of you, and I know you didn't mean anything by it. So don't worry. Bye." Jerry's heart dropped. Pam had heard this. How was he going to explain what happened. *Sorry honey, it was only a crush.* Or, *it didn't mean anything. I love you.* None of these were going to work. He had to think of something and he had to think of something fast, but what could he say?

He tapped lightly on their bedroom door. No answer. He pushed it open and saw Pam packing her suitcase, tears streaming down her cheeks.

"What are you doing?" Jerry's voice wasn't demanding as usual, it was soft and scared, like a little boy watching his mom get the paddle.

"I'm packing, Jerry."

"I know, but why?"

"Because I'm leaving."

"Where you going?"

"I don't know yet. Maybe my sister's for a while, then my mom's. I don't know."

"How long?"

"For good. I can't live with you anymore Jerry. I don't want to be married to you."

Jerry lost it. At first, he started screaming, throwing things, slamming doors, but all this was just making Pam pack faster, along with Gerry and Rachael. After twenty minutes of violence, he started to cry. He was hysterical, falling on his knees, holding her legs, tears streaming down his face, he was moaning, agonizing, wailing. Pam was having a difficult time now, she couldn't look at him, turning her head. She finally got the last bags loaded into their cars, hers and Rachael's, and headed out to her sister's. Pam could see Jerry in the rear view mirror, standing on the front porch, his arms outstretched.

* * * *

James was shivering a little bit. But it was worth it. He had always wanted to Baptize someone in the Ocean, and in January no less. This was the first Baptism since they had moved here. In fact, their first Sunday at Oceanview Fellowship, brought Jeff Phelps and his family to their church. They had come that Sunday and every

Sunday since. Jeff's oldest son Mark, got saved three weeks ago. Jeff, his wife Mary, and Mark were all getting baptized this morning. Jace was really excited, Mark and him had hit it off right away, both starting this year for the Oceanview Tiger Sharks. The Oceanview Tiger Sharks, the name had struck Jace funny. He had lived in the West most of his life, and the mascots were, Grizzlies, Wolves, Stallions, Bulldogs, etc. But out here, it was the Manta Rays, Tiger Sharks, Marlin's, Barracuda's, etc. Jason had already made a big splash with the Sharks, leading them in scoring their first four games before the Holiday break. He helped lead his new team to the number one ranking in State.

Jace had adjusted pretty quickly to his new surroundings, and so had Hannah. James was having a little more difficulty. He still missed some of the people, and it hadn't helped that Principal Gibson and his wife showed up two Sundays ago. Frank's brother lived in a town twenty miles away. James and Hannah had been happy to see them but at the same time, James was saddened. It made him miss Lendel. He did love Oceanview though. The people were friendly and the church was so excited to have him as their Pastor. In the two months he had been there, they had sixteen people join, and this morning they were baptizing three of the six Phelps.

The slight ocean breeze caused James to shiver just a bit. The first week they were there, everyone else was wearing long pants and windbreakers, while the Knoll's were wearing shorts and swimming in the Ocean. James had turned into quite a wimp in two months. He didn't know how he ever made it in the Colorado winters.

Mark stepped into the water first, and James went through the formalities of asking if he was saved. When he brought Mark out of the water there was a huge cheer. It wasn't the few claps that he remembered from Lendel but an explosion of cheer, like at a football game, or basketball game. It was pure joy, and love for the new member of the Oceanview Fellowship family. The same happened with Mary and Jeff. After Jeff and James climbed out of the saltwater and onto the sandy beach, everyone gathered in a circle and sang 'Blest Be the Tie'.

They dismissed and left slowly from the beach. There was no evening service tonight, and the Knolls had planned a big night in

Savannah, Georgia. It was only thirty miles away, and really the only city of any significance nearby. They hadn't been there yet and were excited about going. James hurried home, and took a shower. He hated the way the saltwater felt after it dried on his skin.

* * * *

Bill knocked again, louder than the first time. He had come back from a meeting with his lawyer, and had decided to stop by Adam's house. He had invested quite a bit of money in some land with Adam, and he needed to know if they were close to selling. Right now, he was trying to get his hands on as much cash as possible.

He reached his fist up to knock one more time, but heard some movement in the house. He stopped, waited a minute, putting his hands deep into his coat pockets to keep them warm. He heard the door unlock, and Adam slowly pulled the door open.

"Hey Bill, come on in." A smile came across Adam's face. He opened the door wide.

"Thanks Adam." Bill knocked the snow off his feet and stepped inside quickly. Bill noticed the house was very cool, even after being outside he still got a chill when he stepped in.

"So, how's the case going?" Adam asked over his shoulder. He was leading Bill across the room to where there couch and chairs were set in a way that divided the large front room.

"Not so good. In fact that's part of the reason I'm here. Have we had any lookers on that land up there?" Bill motioned with his head towards the western foothills.

"Yeah, as a matter of fact I got an offer this morning. I was going to call you this evening, but you showed up. The offer is kind of low, but if you're needing some money or something, we could always sell."

"How low?" Adam could hear the concern in Bill's voice.

"We won't lose anything but we certainly aren't going to come out too far ahead."

Bill was relieved. As long as he got back what he had invested, he was going to be happy. "Well what do you think?" He didn't really care what Adam thought, but Adam was the controlling partner.

"I don't want to sell, but if you need the money--"

"I do."

"Well then I guess we'll have to."

"I'm sorry Adam, its just that. . .well. . .the lawyer's fees are adding up, and our credit cards are maxed, and the mortgage is coming up…" Bill's voice trailed off. He had been looking at the carpet the whole time they were talking and he brought his hands to his face, pretending to rub his eyes. He was catching his tears before they hit the floor.

* * * *

Jerry stepped up to his front door, fumbling with his keys. He tucked his gun case under his left arm, dropping the keys on the porch. He bent down to pick them up, and noticed scuff marks on the bottom of the door. This piqued Jerry's curiosity, and he continued looking at them as he stood up. It appeared as if someone had been trying to kick in their front door. There were marks all across the bottom up to about two feet above the porch. He reached out and tried the knob without unlocking the door first. It opened, sticking a bit at the bottom, Jerry had to put a little more effort into pushing it open. He leaned against it hard and it swung wide. He nearly fell over, and barely kept his pistol case from hitting the floor. He was so concerned about his own safety, and the well being of his new treasure he hadn't even noticed the mirror in front of him. Written with soap, in large capital letters was the word JUDAS. He finally stood up coming face to face with himself in the mirror. It took him a second to comprehend the word, but as soon as he did, anger combined with fear overwhelmed him. He opened the case and pulled out his gun letting the case fall to the floor. He held the gun in his right hand, and crouched low to the ground. He moved slowly, keeping himself against the wall, and watching for any type of movement. When he reached a doorway, he would turn the corner quickly, expecting his adversary to be standing there, gun in hand. He eventually made it to his bedroom. He noticed his roll top desk was open and appeared to have been searched through. He looked it over and couldn't find anything missing. He continued searching the house, ending up back at the mirror. He had found no one. No evidence of foul play other than his desk, and the writing on the mirror. He stared at the mirror seeing his face fitting perfectly inside the D. He raised his gun and pointed it at his reflection. He did look tougher, more in command, almost frightening. He liked the way he looked and tried imagining how Candy would feel looking into the barrel of his gun. She probably wouldn't be so arrogant then. Or Pam, or Adam, or James. He wanted to know the fear they would feel, he decided to turn the gun to himself. He placed the barrel against his temple pushing it hard. He tried making himself believe he was actually going to pull the trigger, trying to imagine how the fear would grip them. He moved his index finger back and forth across the trigger guard. Strangely, he wasn't frightened. It didn't bother him at all, even though for a few seconds he thought he might pull the trigger, yet still no fear. Suddenly, the phone rang. Jerry put the gun down and rushed to the phone. I hope its Pam; she's probably going to beg me to take her back. He was wrong.

"Hey Jerry, what's happening?"

Adam's voice sounded more irritating than Jerry had ever thought before. He was tired of hearing him always so happy and giddy. He was sick of him being so trusting. His ego wouldn't even let him consider Jerry as a threat to him in any way and this angered Jerry even more.

"Nothing, how are you Adam?"

"Great! Hey, we just got an offer on our rentals. Can you believe that? We haven't even been thinking about selling them and then all of a sudden someone makes a great offer. I just got off the phone with my parents and Candy's and they are all for it. I was just calling to find out what you think. It will be for about twice what we paid for it."

Jerry was quiet for a minute. He had already sold his dry-cleaners, well it was more like he gave it away selling it so cheap, in fact they were going to be closing on the deal the first of next week. He had planned on just living off the rental income and trying to patch things up with Pam. He hadn't really invested that much in the first place, so he wasn't very excited about selling, even if he was doubling his money.

"Why would we sell though. We'll make double our money in six months anyway."

"Because that's the way the business works. You turn over a profit quickly and move on to the next venture. It's not about the long term anymore, it's the day traders, the era of the internet, satellite, it's a digital world. You gotta move fast. . ."

Jerry didn't hear another word. He knew Adam didn't really care what he thought, he was just calling to be polite. They were going to sell and Jerry had nothing to say about it. He put the phone on his shoulder and picked up the pistol again. He pointed it out the window, and pretended to shoot targets that popped up in his back yard.

." . .okay?"

"Yeah." Jerry said still not paying attention.

"Sunday night after the business meeting. Don't forget."

"I won't."

It was amazing to Jerry how wrapped up people could get with themselves. He had just had a twenty minute conversation with Adam and had only said twenty-two words. He had counted them. The rest of the time Adam had talked non stop, not even pausing for an answer or acknowledgement from Jerry. After a few more boring minutes they reached the "bye's" and hung up their respective phones. Jerry was exhausted from his one-sided conversation and decided to take a little nap. He laid down on the couch, pistol in hand and fell asleep.

Chapter 21

Brad closed his Bible and knelt down to pray. He had always had a decent relationship with Christ, on sometimes--off others, but the last three months had forced him into a total dependence on Christ. Before, he had been able to rely on James, or the strength of the church, or just the fact that things were going good. He now realized how the Apostle Paul could thank God for the trials that were allowed in his life. He had grown considerably, but it was strange how he didn't feel like it. Each day he felt less worthy, less confident in his own abilities and more grateful for the Holy Spirit and the grace of God that allowed him to share his message with these kids. He had also become more aware of the spiritual side of his life. He now understood that he actually did "wrestle not against flesh and blood, but against principalities, against powers, against rulers of the darkness of this world, against spiritual wickedness in high places." He had to come to that realization, before he could ever forgive Jerry, Adam and others. He had to come to that realization before he made his decision to stay. He still struggled sometimes about whether or not he made the right decision, part of him wanted to leave and never set foot in the church that had run off his 'dad', but part of him wanted to stay. Not just for the kids, he knew if he stayed in Lendel, or even in the area, that they would continue to come to his Youth Nights, but because this church was his before it was Adam's. He loved this church, the people in the church, almost as much as he did his family and he would fight for them. He knew James had loved the church too. The church and the community, he loved it so much he left. He knew if he had fought, it would just have torn it apart.

There was one thing Brad sincerely regretted. The Institute. He hadn't told James yet, he had talked to him several times but had conveniently forgot to mention it to him. The Institute was not reopening this next semester. Immediately after James left, the church had stopped supporting the school, and Jerry had called and written all the churches that had supported it, about what was going on. He recommended they withhold their financial support until there was a clear direction for the school. A lot of the churches listened and the school could not afford to operate. They had considered raising tuition, but that would defeat the purpose of the school, so they ended operations after this last semester. Jerry relished this and had even used it to reassure himself and others that they had done the right thing in getting rid of Pastor Knoll.

"See. This was all his idea. If God's hand was on this, wouldn't it still be open?" He didn't realize he sounded like the Jews when they were yelling at Jesus, 'If you're the Son of God, then save yourself'.

Brad finished praying and pushed himself up off the floor. He heard the coffeepot click on. Each morning he had set the timer earlier, so he could drink a cup with his Bible study, and each morning he got up even earlier than what he had expected. Each morning he spent a few minutes more with the Lord.

He glanced in the kitchen as he passed by to see the black coffee dripping into the pot and headed on to Madeline's nursery. He liked to stand by her crib and watch her as she slept while he waited for his coffee to finish. He put his hands on the rail, and was thanking God for this gift when he felt two arms slide around his side and across his chest. He stood there enjoying the hug from his wife, surprised she had gotten up so early. *Some mornings are almost like heaven.* Then the phone rang.

* * * *

Jack sat across the table from Bob. Bob was looking into Jacks eyes, and even though his body was deteriorating, his weight was half what it used to be, he had never seen so much life in Jack's eyes. Here was a man whose life had turned 180 degrees, it was just a pity that it took cancer to do it.

"I want you to have this." Jack said pressing the check into Bob's hand.

Bob was shaking his head and pushing it back. "I can't take this."

Jack had always been stubborn, but now God was using one of his character flaws for His purpose.

"I want to give it to you."

"No, Jack."

Jack's wrinkled eyelids began to twitch, and his large rough hands grabbed Bob's wrist.

"Please, Bob. Don't take this blessing away from me." He put the check in Bob's hand one more time and watched him close his fingers around it. "Now we got that settled, how 'bout you ordering some food. You're gonna waste away."

Bob laughed. If he didn't eat from now until next January he would still probably weigh more than Jack did now.

"Alright. I'll get something."

They ordered their food by number and got fresh cups of coffee.

"Jack," Bob interrupted their silence, "What do you think about demons?"

"I think they're bad." They both laughed. "No seriously, I think they exist. I think they are probably around us more than either of us realize."

"Do you think they can bother Christians?"

"I suppose." Jack answered.

"Do you think they might hang out, like, I don't know, maybe set up residency or something?"

"You mean pick out a certain person and give em the heebee-geebees, or try to make 'em sin?"

"Yeah, kinda." Bob agreed.

"Well I might not be the best person to ask about this. I didn't study Demonology at Spiritual U, but I guess they probably could, if God allowed them to."

That made sense to Bob, but also made him a little more curious. "Why would God allow them to?"

"It might be the only way he could git your attention, or fir some it might be reassurance, kinda like if you're not facin' the fire, you're not in the fight. Maybe there's somethin' your allowin' in your life that keeps them there." Jack sat back as the waitress set down their plates. "Do you think you're bein' bothered by demons?"

"I know I am."

* * * *

"Okay then, see you in a few minutes." Brad hung up the phone.

"Who was that?" Jenny asked.

"Alysha."

"Alysha?" "Yeah she said she needs to talk to us."

"Right now?" Jenny was looking at the clock as she asked.

"I guess so."

Alysha Stevenson had come to their church the last three years. Her parents had left when rumors had begun surfacing about James. Apparently, they had gone through this at another church before they moved to Lendel, and they did not want to deal with it again. Alysha hadn't been very involved in the youth and it wasn't a surprise she hadn't been back after they left. It was surprising she was calling them now and this early.

Jenny went to the bathroom and tried getting at least a little ready. Brad just threw on a pair of jeans, T-shirt, and hat. He got his cup of coffee and poured himself a bowl of cereal to get him started before Alysha got there.

Jenny was just coming out of their bedroom when the doorbell rang.

"Hurry and get that before Madeline wakes up."

Brad jumped up and rushed over to the door.

"Hey Alysha come on in."

She came in and Brad took her coat. They went into the kitchen to sit at the table.

"Do you want a cup of coffee or some cereal or something?" Jenny asked.

Alysha shook her head. She looked bad. Her eyes were swollen from crying and there was a very evident bruise on her cheek bone. She was chewing on her hair and hadn't made eye contact the entire time she had been in their house.

"So Alysha, what's up?" Brad had never been good at letting people volunteer information.

She continued chewing on her hair. "I'm pregnant."

"Have you told your parents?" Brad wasn't trying to sound cold, he had already anticipated this was what she was coming by for, and unfortunately, he had a lot of experience in counseling on this issue. It was critical to find out if the parents knew or not.

"I haven't talked to my parents since I moved out."

"You moved out? When was that?"

"Two months ago. I moved in with my boyfriend."

Jenny had stopped what she was doing and had moved over to the table with them. "Is that who hit you?"

Alysha nodded.

Brad could feel himself getting mad. But his anger was toward Adam. He felt like this was his fault. He had pushed these people away from their church. If they had still been there this might have never happened. But why was it toward Adam? Normally in these situations, his anger would have been kindled toward Jerry. Then the realization hit him.

* * * *

Jerry jumped from his sleep. He looked at the clock. It was 2:15. In the morning? Afternoon? He couldn't get his mind to work right. He saw a shadow move across the window and his fear sobered his mind quickly. It was night. He had fallen asleep on the couch hours ago, but had woke from sleep in total fear. It was his dream. Now reality was almost as frightening. He reached for the gun that was already in his hand, and that calmed his fear somewhat. He was watching the window when he heard a heavy knock on the door. His heart began pounding, *this could be it.* He took a deep breath and walked nervously toward the door. A second knock hurried his steps somewhat, and he now tried hiding his right hand behind his back, concealing the pistol. He looked out the peephole and saw a police officer standing there. Jerry opened the door quickly.

"Is everything alright sir?" The officer asked looking past Jerry, his eyes scanning the house.

"Uh, yeah I guess. Why?"

"You don't know sir?"

"Know what?"

"Do you mind if we come in for a second and take a look around?"

Jerry hadn't even noticed the other two officers standing behind this one.

"Uh no. Come on in. What are you looking for?"

The first two officers pushed by and began looking around the house, the third stayed with Jerry.

"There was a 911 call placed from this residence ten minutes ago. What are you doing with that?"

Jerry looked down at his hand to see the pistol.

"I-I was sleeping and something woke me up. I grabbed my gun because I saw something moving in the window."

"Oh, so you called 911?"

"No. I've been asleep." Jerry didn't notice the officer's right hand resting on the butt of his gun.

"So if you didn't place the call who did?"

Jerry stopped to think on this for a minute. "I don't know." He had been so engrossed in thought he didn't hear the officer unsnap the guard on his holster.

"You don't know?"

"No." Jerry was getting agitated. He felt like the officer was condemning him.

He lifted his hand to shut the door. Unfortunately, it was the hand his gun was in. The officer drew his gun.

"STOP!" the officer screamed, his gun leveling on Jerry's face.

Jerry dropped his gun and threw his hands in the air. The other two officers came rushing into the room. The officer with his gun on Jerry motioned him to turn around.

"Put your hands behind your back!"

Jerry complied. He felt the cuffs tighten around his wrist, cutting into his skin. The officer grabbed the center of the cuffs.

"What's going on?" Jerry heard the first officer ask.

"He tried to pull a gun on me."

"He did?"

"Yeah."

The first officer walked around to look at Jerry.

"Can you tell me what went on here tonight?"

Jerry looked up at the officer, he was trying not to seem nervous, thinking that might give the wrong impression. "Nothing sir. I just fell asleep, and then got woke up by a noise. I looked out the front window and saw something move across it. Next thing I knew, you guys were knocking on the door. That's it."

"So you didn't call 911?"

"No, sir."

"Is there anyone else in the house?"

"No."

"You're married aren't you? Where's your wife?"

"She's at her mom's." Jerry said mournfully.

"Well the phone in your bedroom was off the hook, and there were papers and bills thrown everywhere. Are you sure you didn't call."

Jerry's mind was racing. *So some one was in the house. I'm not just going crazy.*

"I'm sure, sir."

"Alright, now what's this business about pulling a gun on my officer?"

Jerry went on to explain what had happened, and the police officers seemed understanding. Jerry could be quite a salesman when he had to be. The officers finally turned to leave, reminding Jerry they would be watching him. He thanked them, and closed the door as they left. He sat down on the couch. He was trying to remember what it was that really woke him. It wasn't a noise, it wasn't the cold, it was his dream. The dream he had been having for a while now. The dream of all the deacons sitting around a table and Satan leading the meeting. He had never really got a good look at the devil's face until tonight, but for the life of him, he couldn't remember whose face it was. He remembered being terrified when he first saw it, but also not shocked at all. Almost like he expected it, but who was it? He tried putting different peoples faces in it, but none fit. He tried James, then Bob, Jack, Phillip, Steve, Brad, and even Candy's but none fit. It was Cinderella's slipper.

Chapter 22

The Sunday morning service was pleasant, Brad thought, as pleasant as it could be. Pleasant but not meaningful. He looked around the auditorium and saw far more empty seats than full. One nice surprise was Alysha. He had been praying for her ever since she had come by his house. He was seriously contemplating bringing up her situation at the meeting tonight, but decided no one would care since her parents didn't come, and therefore didn't tithe. Tithe. That's what the meeting would be about most likely. It wouldn't be about the pains, the hurts, the prayer requests, the praises, but just the fact they needed a Pastor so the people would have a reason to tithe. How far they had fallen since James left. Business meetings were more like testimony and prayer meetings with James, but now they were like school board meetings, or judicial hearings.

Brad looked around the auditorium. He took out a piece of paper and grabbed the pen from the pen holder on the pew in front of him. He decided he would write down one prayer request for each person in the church. He started on the far right. He didn't know the real struggles of each person, only the surface ones. The ones the people let show through so no one would try to dig deeper. He prayed for Ben's daughter, and her rocky marriage not realizing Ben was in over his head at work. Right now, he was dealing with the fact he might have to foreclose on this church. His struggle with this was putting a strain on his relationship with his wife, and a dagger in his faith in God. He prayed for Bill knowing he was blamed for an accident at the mill, not having any idea that he had been embezzling for months. He prayed for Jack to have peace while he was going through the pain, and for their money not to be drained allowing Janice some to survive on, not realizing Jack was a multi-millionaire and happier than he had been in the previous sixty-seven years of his life. He didn't realize that Jack had never tithed and was making up for that these last three months. He didn't realize that every time the church was cutting a missionaries support, Jack was picking up that missionary personally and doubling their support. He prayed for Bob, and his discipling of Principal Gibson, not realizing he was facing the same attacks and spiritual conflict Brad was. He continued through the people of Lendel Community Church saying a brief prayer for each one of them, and then jotting down his prayer list. He got to the end and felt better about the service. It wasn't much longer and the interim they had this week ended in prayer. He gave a brief invitation, and like every week, no one went forward.

Brad and Jenny headed into the hall and saw the deacons and Adam heading toward the Pastor's office. Brad knew they were probably planning their strategy for the business meeting tonight. He shook his head and holding Madeline in one arm, grabbed Jenny's arm with the other and headed to their car.

Adam grabbed Ben's arm and held him back as the men headed into the office.

"I tried calling you this week."

"Yeah, I've been real busy at the bank."

"I bet. There's a lot of stuff going on. What I was trying to get a hold of you on is that we have a buyer for our cleaning biz."

"I didn't know we were selling." Ben answered.

"Me either, it just kind of came out of the blue. He's offering us almost double what we paid. That's pretty good."

"Yeah. To be honest Adam I don't really care what we do."

"Then you're willing to sell."

"Sure."

"Great, I'll let him know, and you'll probably have a check by Thursday."

They shook hands with Adam's prompting, and headed in the office to join the other men. They were sitting in chairs around the desk, and Adam was left the seat behind it. Adam called the meeting to order and began immediately planning out strategies. This frustrated Jerry. He was the speaker, he was the one supposed to be in charge, and here was Adam, not even a deacon, trying to take over *his* meeting. He shifted in his chair. He had brought his pistol to church, and had shoved it in his waist band behind his back. He didn't know why he had brought it, but it made him feel more powerful, a different kind of power. Not power that everyone saw, but that he felt himself. It made him smile to know no one knew he had the gun. Right now, though it was uncomfortable and Adam continuing to talk wasn't helping the situation. Jerry finally stood up.

"Yes Jerry?" Adam said looking at him intently.

Jerry shifted his feet. Adam's gaze was making him feel uncomfortable, and the longer Adam looked at him the smaller Jerry felt.

"Oh nothing, I just was a little uncomfortable sitting here."

"No Jerry, if you had something to say then say it."

Jerry hadn't wanted to say anything but now he did. He felt prompted. "Okay. I think we are making a huge mistake. I think we need to call someone in as an interim to get us straightened out. I agree with Bob." *Where is this coming from. I don't want an interim.* "I don't know, maybe we should consider someone that's already here. I've preached some before, and I know both Adam and Bill have--"

Ben interrupted Jerry. "I had felt the same way as you Jerry, but there is something you guys need to know. The bank is probably going to have to foreclose on this church. I don't know why we haven't made our payments--"

Jerry jumped in. "Why wasn't I told of this sooner? I'm the speaker."

Adam laughed. Jerry turned to him, hate burning in his eyes. *What are you laughing at?* he thought. "I am!" He said angrily.

Adam smiled widely. "Sure you are Jerry. Sure you are. Just as much as you are a great business man, or a good father, or is it an adulterous father."

"What are you talking about?!" Jerry screamed.

Adam continued smiling. "You don't know? Do you think it was any accident I was out of town that night? Don't you see Jerry, I pulled your strings that night, just as I have when you're in the pulpit. Do you really think anyone would have wanted you to lead the church? Everything you've done, I've done for you."

Jerry was enraged, he was looking around the room, and all he saw were blank faces staring back. No reaction, no surprise, and just then it hit him. His dream. The face. It was Adam's. Adam was the one leading the meeting. Jerry felt sick. He thought about grabbing the gun, but instead he headed for the door.

"Jerry where you going?" Bill asked as he stood to grab him.

"Let him go," Adam said coldly. Bill sat down.

Jerry rushed out of the office and down the hall. He sprinted across the parking lot and got in his car. He headed home, not caring for his safety, swerving in and out of traffic. *How could I have been so deceived. I ran off our Pastor, my friend. I listened to Adam. I lost my family. So deceived.* Jerry got to his house and ran up the steps and through the front door. He picked up the phone to call his wife, but no answer. *She's probably at church.* He headed back to his roll top desk and sat in the chair. He pulled out a pen and a notepad and started to write. He had never kept a journal, he hadn't even written a letter before, but this was going to be a combination. Part letter, part journal. He wanted to see, in writing, where his life had taken the wrong turn. The flag of pain and anguish flew high on his mast now.

* * * *

James looked across his congregation. Everyone was turning in their seats to kneel against the pews. James knelt too. There had been a lot of prayer requests tonight, and James had made one himself. Jerry. He didn't know why but he had felt compelled to pray for Jerry. Even after the wonderful service they had today, and the love gift the church had given him, James still felt a little down today, all because of Jerry.

As people began praying, all self -prompted, James thanked God for leading him to this congregation. It was the perfect place for him to heal, plus hearing each and every person giving a heartfelt prayer for a man they didn't even know, that was amazing.

* * * *

Bob held the door for two young couples, then hurried down the sidewalk to help Mrs. Green across the slippery cement. He was surprised so many people were turning out for this business meeting, especially with the ice storm they were having. Usually they cancelled services when the weather was like this, but not tonight. He was holding Mrs. Green's arm, and looked back just in time to see Hank Peters big old four-wheel drive slide past the parking lot, narrowly missing the telephone pole. Hank backed it up slowly, and got it parked.

Bob pulled the front door open for Mrs. Green and they could feel the heat pour out of the church, instantly turning cold. He waited by the door for Hank, and helped him in pulling the door tight, trying to keep the wind from pulling it open. Bill was going to keep an eye out until the services started.

Brad passed by, stopping long enough to shake Bob's hand.

"Have you seen Jerry?"

"No. He hasn't come in since I've been here." Bob answered.

"I tried calling his house twenty minutes ago but didn't get an answer. I hope he didn't get in a wreck or something."

"Oh, he'll be here. They just might have to start without him though."

Brad smiled and nodded, passing on to the auditorium. Bob waited about ten more minutes, then he heard the congregation start singing. He took one last look out across the parking lot, and not seeing anyone out there, he headed to the auditorium. He stepped in to see the auditorium was about half full. That was more than had been there the last two Sunday mornings. It was a bit of an encouragement.

Bob's eyes searched out his wife and he hustled into the seat next to her. He joined in on the third verse of a not-so-familiar hymn, and struggled with the chorus. They had a short prayer, were seated, and then Adam took the stage.

"Good evening."

"Good evening." Came the broken, non-unison, response.

"Well I'm glad to see all of you that decided to brave Mother Nature. She certainly didn't want us here tonight."

There were a few courtesy chuckles.

"We have several things to go over tonight, so I guess we need to get started. Jerry will probably get here any minute, but until then, I'll go ahead and take his place.

The first order of business, is our church loan. Ben will update us on what is going on in this area. Ben." Adam held his hand out to Ben.

Ben looked a lot older, as he struggled to get out of his pew, and he even needed Adam's help to get up the stairs onto the platform. Bob noted that he seemed to have aged twenty-five years in the last two weeks.

"As you know, I am a Senior Officer at the Tri-County Bank. I sit on the board that granted this church its loan, eight years ago. The church has been so faithful in its payments, and have even been on pace to pay it off in half the years, but over the last six months, payments have not been made. The bank wishes to proceed with foreclosure. I have argued and fought with the board, but after many Notifications of Delinquency certificates have been issued, and no response was offered, I had no choice but to side with the board. We have until Thursday of next week to bring our balance current or we will be evicted."

Several hands shot up right away. Ben acknowledged the closest.

"Why was there no response, and why weren't we notified earlier?"

Ben looked toward Adam for the answer.

"We don't know exactly." Adam said, trying to look as concerned as possible. "We think they were over looked with all the other things that were going on, and tossed in the trash, or maybe some one was taking them, I just don't know. However, believe me, your deacon board only found out about this, a few hours ago. We were just as shocked as you."

"How much do we owe?" Jack asked.

"To bring us current, I believe it's just a little over $50,000.00."

There was a gasp in the crowd, then total silence.

"And when do we have to have this by." Jack asked again. He had no intention of letting this church get foreclosed, and as long as he had the finances, he would keep it's testimony intact.

"Thursday of next week."

There was some more discussion on this subject but Bob was more concerned about Jerry. He kept looking out the windows every time he saw headlights, but it was never Jerry. They finally moved onto another subject. Missions.

After spending about twenty minutes, trying to decide which Missionaries to keep and which to cut, Principal Gibson stood up.

"Now that we are on the subject of Missions, I think its time we discuss some of our home missions. Actually, I just want to discuss one. The Institute. I know some people decided it wasn't our responsibility to keep it open, but it is our responsibility to help as much as we can, and let people know how valuable it is. Brad is just one of many graduates from there, who have gone on to wonderful ministries. But even beyond this, do you know what it could do to the economy to pull out more than eight hundred students. I know some of you probably don't think it will do much, but it has some of the local business people worried. Especially the fast food and laundry mat owners. It could end up being a chain reaction." Frank cleared his throat before continuing. "Do you realize crime has gone down since the Institute moved in? People are proud of it, many elderly take walks through the campus, and every year it increases in size. Can you even fathom how many lives have been changed because of this school. Lives that might not have ever been touched, because of financial or travel burdens. I know the price of a higher education, I deal with it almost everyday, and there has never been a school as affordable, and as high quality as the Mountain View Bible Institute. I believe we need to reevaluate our decision of cutting our finances for this Mission."

Bob felt like a proud father. Frank had grown so much and so fast, it was hard to believe he had only been a Christian for a few months.

Adam approached the microphone again. "I wish Jerry were here. He has a lot of good numbers and facts about the school. I appreciate your input Frank, and you made some good points. However, I feel we should wait until our next meeting to make any decisions about the school, that way both sides could have ample time to prepare. Well if there are no other comments we need to get moving along."

And move along they did. Adam covered quite a few topics that night, all very brief. He never even gave any chance for a rebuttal or questions from anyone in the audience. Finally, and mercifully, the meeting was dismissed. Bob got up looking for Jerry, but he was no where to be seen. He was worried. There was no way Jerry would miss something like this.

* * * *

Sitting on the edge of his bed, Jerry heard the phone ring. *Maybe it's Pam,* he thought. He let the voice mail get it. He looked in the dresser mirror again, having a hard time making eye contact with himself. He had turned all the photographs smiling at him from the dresser top, face down. All that could be seen was his face, and his letter/journal. He had taped it, page by page, across the top of the mirror.

He shook his head violently, trying to rid himself of the images of James, sitting there crying with him at the hospital, of Bob standing as his best man at his wedding, of him trying to kiss Candy, of Adam standing in front of the microphone, of Rachael with a beer can in her hand, and of Pam's tail lights as she drove away. But the worst, the most fearful was Pam's face when he said he had gone through the drive-thru for his supper. The instant he ridded himself of one image two new ones took its place. It was unmerciful, never ending.

He was rocking back and forth on the edge of his bed, holding his gun in both hands, hanging it between his knees. Twice he had brought it up underneath his chin, but both times, he had backed down. The screams were getting louder, and the scenes were coming faster. He tried closing his eyes, but that did nothing for him. Finally, he closed his eyes, opened his mouth and let his gun barrel rest on his tongue. At first the taste of old gun smoke mixed with metal made him gag, but after just a couple seconds, it seemed to calm the scenes. His mind became peaceful, the bombarding ended. He now knew his destination and had come to peace with it. He pulled the hammer back on the pistol and decided to count to five. He would pull the trigger at three.

*One……two……*the door bell rang. Jerry stopped for a minute opening his eyes. *Oh, go away. You'll only be sorry if you come in here.* He listened to see if he could hear a car leave, or the doorbell again. Nothing.

One……two……

"Jerry! Jerry!, are you home?"

What is Bob doing here. Jerry was trying to think. He pulled the pistol out of his mouth, and tried shoving it under the covers but Bob stepped in two seconds too soon.

"Jerry! There you are. I've been looking all over for you…What are you doing with that?" As soon as Bob asked the question, he was figuring out the answer. He saw the letter taped to the mirror, he saw the pictures turned over on the dresser, and he saw the tears in Jerry's eyes. Jerry was sitting on the edge of his bed, trembling.

"I-I…I don't know." Jerry spoke so softly it was almost inaudible.

Bob didn't know what to do. He said a quick prayer asking for guidance, moving next to Jerry on the bed. He put his arm around him and Jerry crumbled in the big man's arms. He began sobbing, wailing, he cried every tear he had, and then just made the sounds. This was a broken man.

"Thank you for caring enough to come look for me." Jerry finally said after his thirty minutes of anguish.

"Jerry, I would have driven all the way to Taiwan if you needed me too…How did it get this far?" Bob's question wasn't directed toward Jerry, but was asked in general. Jerry still answered.

"I don't know exactly, but a lot of it is up there on the mirror."

Bob looked up at the letter taped to the glass. He pulled the papers off and began reading. There was no one major turning point, just a common theme. Bob could see how easily his life could be where Jerry's is now. How easily the roles could have been reversed. He finished the letter, and laid it down on the end of the bed.

Jerry began talking. "I should have made a stand. I knew things weren't right, I knew the motives of many were not pure, my own wife begged me to stop. Why didn't I listen? Why was I so easily led astray? Was it ego? Greed? I should have stood up for what was right."

Bob had nothing to say. He wanted to encourage Jerry but the words didn't come.

"Do you think it's too late for me?. . .Do you think I've fallen too far away, to be able to make any difference now?"

"No. But it's not going to be easy."

"Bob. Would you pray with me?"

Bob nodded, and both men knelt at the foot of Jerry's bed. He had never heard a prayer like Jerry's before. He might never again.

After Jerry's outpouring of his heart, and Bob's prayer, Jerry stood to his feet.

"I think I need to call James."

"Are you sure?"

"Yeah." Jerry said wiping away a few more tears. "Do you have his number?"

Bob searched through his wallet, and found the number scribbled on the back of an old business card. Jerry thanked him and dialed the number.

"Hello." James voice had a healing effect on Jerry's soul.

"Hi James this is Jerry. Do you have a couple minutes?"

* * * *

Pam was really dreading tonight. After the last five months, she just wanted some time away, to think things through. She wondered if her decision had been the most prudent one, but Jerry had sounded so sincere on the phone. From the start of their conversation, Pam knew there was something different about him. She could hear the joy that used to pervade his life, all the way through the phone lines. She could even hear his smile when she agreed to meet him at The Eatery in Frisco. Now she was somewhat nervous as the lights of Frisco filled her view. She hated to doubt her husband's sincerity, and as she pulled up to the diner, she no longer did. There was her husband. There was the man she had married. She could see it on his face, she could see it in his walk, and as soon as she approached him, she could feel it in his touch. She had told herself she would not even let him touch her, but that quickly changed.

"Pam. I missed you."

Without a word, Pam wrapped her arms around his neck, squeezing tighter when she felt him return the embrace with equal love.

"I missed you too," she whispered.

* * * *

Adam slid the 'SOLD' label into the slot on the sign in front of their house. He took a deep breath, shook his head, and climbed into their packed moving van. He started the engine and turned down the road headed for the highway. Candy was sitting next to him, her atlas in hand.

"Well, do you know where we are headed yet?"

Adam smiled. "Not for sure, but I hear South Carolina is nice this time of year."

Printed in the United States
744800001B

9 781588 512208